*
**

Acosmos
&
The Story Lovers

Homage to Roland Barthes

***

Mike Gane

Copyright © 2024 M. J. Gane

The moral right of the author has been asserted.

Photo on cover: Donna Velata (la Fede?) by Antonio Corradini (1752).
Wikimedia: Creative Commons [Sailko].

The resemblance of any person, idea, event, depicted
in this work to any actual person, idea, event is
purely coincidental. This work must not be lent, resold, hired
out or otherwise circulated without the author's prior consent in any form
of binding or cover other than that in which it is herein presented and without
a similar condition including this condition being imposed on the subsequent reader.

Troubador Publishing Ltd
Unit E2 Airfield Business Park
Harrison Road, Market Harborough
Leicestershire LE16 7UL
Tel: 0116 279 2299
Email: books@troubador.co.uk
Web: www.troubador.co.uk

ISBN 978 1805143 741

British Library Cataloguing in Publication Data.
A catalogue record for this book is available from the British Library.

Printed and bound in Great Britain by 4edge Limited
Typeset in 11pt Minion Pro by Troubador Publishing Ltd, Leicester, UK

*He said… it is as if I remember the stories themselves
without their story
She said… but they do have a story.*

…

Prescriptum

It should perhaps remain a mystery how these pieces of fiction came to be assembled. Even then, was there a manuscript? Evidently each fragment is self-contained, and I have added the numbering to the chronology, which was easy to establish. The order on the pages is to be explained by the fact that Acosmos had a companion who remained in strict anonymity as X. For each story exchange the two story tellers agreed to read a "fragment" from Barthes' book and for this to influence in some way the story told, and to include one word agreed in advance in each of the stories exchanged (the kigo word): the order of reading these is given in Contents II. I have edited the stories by eliminating extraneous or rambling or incoherent sentences, several interruptions and limited each micro story to 230 words in line with the wishes of Giorgio Acosmos.

(Mike Gane, Editor, 2023)

Contents

Part 1	Summer			1
1.	Venus	Haiku I	Haiku II	3
2.	On the Train			4
3.	Monk and Nun			6
4.	Going Somewhere			8
5.	Miracle			10
Part 2	Autumn			13
6.	Dreams	Haiku I	Haiku II	15
7.	Weep			16
8.	Rendezvous			18
9.	Karma			20
10.	Palindrome			22
11.	Representation			24
12.	Love			26
13.	Walled Garden			28
14.	Assonance			30
15.	Library			32
16.	Object of Desire			34
Part 3	Winter			39
17.	Question	Haiku I	Haiku II	41
18.	Viper			42
19.	Collecting			44
20.	Contrasts			46
21.	Shooting			48

Contents[1]

22.	Circles	50
23.	Subject and Object	52
24.	Figments	54
25.	Bounced	56
26	Personal Time	58
Part 4	Spring	61
27.	Feminism	64
28.	Finale	66
29.	Veer Off	68
30.	Transgenic	70
31.	Disconnect	72
32.	The Meal	74
33.	Eclectic	76
Part 5	The Conference	79
34.	Guardian	82
35.	Homage	84
36.	New Lexicon	86
37.	Games	88
38.	Legs	90
39.	Passion	92
40.	Performance	94
41.	Pleasure	96
42.	Falsification	98

---

1 These titles were added by the editor after the collection was complete.

Part 6	Autumn and Winter			101
43.	Realignment	Haiku I	Haiku II	103
44.	Clues			104
45.	Words			106
46.	On the Other Side			108
47.	Phantoms			110
48.	Boy			112
49.	The Writer			114
50.	A Last Exchange			116
Part 7	The Ending			119
51.	Scatter	Haiku I	Haiku II	121
52.	Death			122
Part 8	Coda			125
53.	Haiku I	Haiku II		125

Addendum: A Short Note on the Storytelling	127
Bibliography	130
Contents II	132

Part I

5 June – 4 July 1993

Summer

Carpe Fabula

*"There is a certain art in receiving a telephone call,"
said the old man sitting next to me on the train. "For
years I have played a certain game. I try to judge the
psychology of the caller by letting the phone ring. After
a certain length of time I know if I had been the caller
I would have stopped ringing. I am sure then that I
have the upper hand psychologically and pick up the
phone. If I have just missed the caller I am sometimes
thrown – paradoxically – into a deep depression. But
this is the risk of the game," he said. At that moment
his mobile phone began to ring. Without a moment's
hesitation he answered. "Wrong number," he said. "I
should have waited," he murmured nervously. "I get
wrong numbers three or four times a day." He looked
out of the window. He then said, "You can't really have
a dialogue with a wrong number, though I have tried
from time to time."*[2]

---

[2] It seems likely that this impromptu story by X started the idea of telling stories to Acosmos who kept a rough annotated copy of it later entitled "X's Challenge". It is dated early June, 1993. Acosmos evidently believed they had met before, as he appended a poem from 1877 by Afanasy Fet: "And many years pass... And Lo, your voice arrives again one silent night/ And as before, the wonder of your sounds/ Reveals that you alone are Life, that you alone are love."

1

Friday, 5 June 1993[3]

Acosmos begins:

On the cliff's edge
Of an adventure
The gentle abyss of bright stars

-X- says:

> *Through silvery mists*
> *Repose of the abyssal valley*
> *A fabula gratulatoria*

---

[3] The exchanges began with these two haikai. These were handwritten and dated. The one by X also had in quotes the phrase 'I succumb' evidently taken from the figure *s'abimer*. The *tabula gratulatoria* is not included in the English version of Barthes' *Fragments d'un Discours Amoureux* (1977); *A Lover's Discourse: Fragments* (1978). There was also a short note saying that the stories should be prepared but delivered as improvisations, not as texts therefore but as librettos; not as monologues but duologues or heterologues.

On the Train.

X

Friday, 11 June 1993

…a young woman got into the train and sat opposite a dignified intellectual-looking man in his early 50s wearing a clerical collar. They had already exchanged haikai a week before. "I'll begin," he said. […] "They both had a passion for writing fiction and in Fragments d'un discourse amoureux *(Barthes) so they began to exchange short stories – they called 'micros'. They had met by chance one day in the city and became story exchangers during a lunch break. […] After an unfortunate syllepsis and conversion there was a pause in their relationship. Later they met again and decided to renew their pact: let us begin again they said.[4] But it was never the same, they became somewhat aggressive to each other's fictions. The story lovers continued for a while and then decided to end it with a final exchange: each would write a kigo-haiku."[5] The woman thought for a moment and said, "I'm taken aback by your collar, a real sartor resartus.[6] I find your story interesting, the end is foretold but life is full of surprises. I am honoured to be in your story…" The train slowed. There was an announcement: "There will be an unscheduled delay. We apologise for the inconvenience." She smiled. "You see, your fiction has already had a consequence, we have more time."*

---

4   In X's handwriting there is an insertion into the story at this point: "There was a brief contract at the beginning concerning privacy, commitment to fictional experiment, and one or two strange references to love and to the poetry of Ted Hughes."

5   In the Japanese tradition the kigo word bonds with the season, here it bonds the two stories.

6   Reference to Thomas Carlyle's 1838 novel of that name, possibly translated as the tailor reclothed. It is a biography of a German philosopher based on the evidence of assorted fragments received in six paper bags.

2

…it was a late evening train, back from the metropolis to the midlands on a Friday. As the train picked up speed, and as the passengers settled into the journey a mobile phone rang. A businessman found his phone, and, in a voice clearly audible to the whole of the compartment said, "No, I'm free to talk, there's no one listening. I love you, *cherie*. I'm sorry I'm having to leave for the weekend." He then picked up his pen and took down a telephone number. He said, "I must ring off, we are about to go into a long tunnel, we'll be cut off anyway." And before he put the phone away, he said, "I love you, here it is, *au revoir*," and there followed an interminable tunnel. The businessman waited, impatiently, till the train emerged. He then phoned someone to say he would be home soon – "I love you, darling." and began to think about acosmic philosophy and his Journal of Business Affairs. His eyes closed. He fell asleep. He missed his station and rendezvous, and was woken up at the end of the line and prophetic dream. "*Omnis determinatio est negatio*" he said to himself.[7]

---

[7] *Omnis determinatio est negatio* (Spinoza, 1674) is the slogan of acosmism (see Sartre *Being and Nothingness,* ch 1).

Monk and Nun.

Thursday, 17 June 1993

…"I would like to talk about allegory," said the literary analyst. "It suggests of course as everyone knows that meaning is twofold. A direct and manifest meaning, and an indirect even hidden meaning of reference." He paused. "Thus a story about a monk and a nun could be about you and I," he said, looking with a smile at the woman. "Its etymology suggests it is made up of 'other' and 'speaking' through the text." "So, if I tell a story about X and Y and if it is possible to read this in terms of A and B this is allegory. But what about metaphor?" "Well," said the analyst, "the etymology of metaphor is from 'change' and 'to bear' and implies a shift to relations which would not usually carry the meaning" She reflected on this briefly then asked, "Is this story itself an allegory?" "Perhaps," said the analyst. "What am I?" she asked. "Fabulous, a fabula," he replied. "What if the two are joined together?" "I call it zeugma. But it's an unconventional relationship in an innocent but devoted discourse," he replied.

3

-X-

...I once took a walk through the fields trying to avoid a monastery near by. But I encountered a monk on a lonely path. I said, "Good morning, do you mind if I say that I've been thinking a lot recently about changing my lifestyle, to becoming a nun in fact. I'm not a deeply intellectual kind of Christian. I don't have a great and wide knowledge of the scriptures. But I would like to spend the rest of my life in such a study. However, I have never seen any account of how one becomes a nun. Of course, there are no advertisements for various competing orders, the various advantages and disadvantages. I know that some monks seem to have a reputation for being bon viveurs and even for making their own liqueurs. But others have a rather dour style." At this point the monk nodded and smiled and departed. Probably a devoted Trappist, I concluded. Good at non-verbal interlocution. I saw joy shooting from his eyes. I wonder if my last word might be the vow of chastity and silence.

Going Somewhere.

Monday, 28 June 1993

X begins…

> *…and there are many bizarre pastimes. I became aware of one of the most strange when I encountered someone photographing thunderstorms. He explained that he was suffering from anxiety, and attracted to two things: beautiful women and lightning. First he had tried to snap women and lightning. He had learnt that before lightning strikes, strange electric feelers reach up towards the lightning and trace out in advance a path for it to follow down to earth. Only rarely had this been captured on film. And even in these cases the lightning had "chosen" to follow another trailer and "rejected" the one caught on camera. He had two cameras ready in this particular storm: the one he was pointing towards the sky, the other some paces back held by his attractive companion pointed strangely towards him. She saw the flashing thunder and lightning approaching: don't be anxious anymore. "My ultimate hope," he said, "is to be chosen."*

4

Acosmos says,

> …On a long voyage through seas and oceans I once met an interesting elderly man. It was in a shady part of a deck with a clear view of calm blue sea and sky. I can't remember how the conversation began, but I soon became aware this particular man was unusual. He thought in dramatic contrasts and oppositions, yet sometimes his lines of thought were strangely inverted. In the middle of one conversation he simply announced that perhaps because I was a woman I had misunderstood him and had got the whole point upside down. On another occasion I thought he was talking about America but it became clear from the content he was talking about Europe. I asked him, at one of our exchanges, where he was bound for. "I have been travelling very many years from the East," he said. "But you are the first woman ever to ask me about my final destination." He turned to the distant horizon, pointed out to sea, and said, "I'm seeking the West Pole, come to me… swept away by anxiety and a fear of danger you are the chosen one." I remembered certain lines from Sartor Resartus… "Was the attraction mutual; pole and pole trembling towards contact…?"[8] […]

---

8   Carlyle, *Sartor Resartus*, ch 5.

Miracle.

Monday, 5 July 1993

…a woman received a message from a male friend. It came as a complete surprise because although there had been a close friendship between them some years back it had faded. She had made it plain that she had been attracted to him. The message suggested that they meet 'for a drink, perhaps a snack or a meal'. When they met in a restaurant the man told her he had reorganised and rethought his life; a new job (a different firm), a change of apartment, some new clothes. He wanted quite simply to get to know a wider circle of acquaintances: at fifty-one should have a renaissance. He had brought a red rose and gave it to her. […] "What are your intentions?" she asked directly. "I've decided to relax, enjoy life and find pleasure wherever I can," he said. "Does that mean you are or are not looking for a new romance?" she asked. "Only if it is in the logic of pleasure," he replied philosophically. "Is there a 'logic of pleasure'?" asked the woman. "Surely," she continued, "there are pacts but without a logic. And what's more it would be a miracle if these pacts were not more violent, passionate and energetic than a genteel logic of pleasure would suggest." She paused. "OK, let's go into the logic of pleasure; it's consensual," she said. "If I can bring the pleasure of logic – and perhaps imagine new '*Fragments*' beyond hedonism," he replied. She paused, looked at the rose, reflected, "To be a kept secret between us" she said.

5

X

…It had been an unusually hot summer. One memory lingered. One day the sun beat down without mercy on the mile-long sandy beach on which a vast multitude of people were lying elbow to elbow. At the water's edge were hundreds of parents playing with their children. Further into the water were adults swimming and playing games of various kinds. There was no wind save for hint of an on-shore breeze. […] Suddenly virtually all of the sunbathers stood up and went into the water leaving the beach empty apart from the new friends. Everyone noticed the fact, talked about it, tried to explain it. "An amazing chance occurrence, just imagine that!" said a mathematician who was in the water. "Statistically it is possible that at one moment, by chance, a large number of people suddenly decide to do the same thing." Everyone agreed a most rare and precious event had taken place. An extreme coincidence which may take place once a lifetime taken as a sign by the couple they had an elective and exclusive affinity; a pact: they had witnessed and experienced an inconsequential miracle, but "From what, seeing them, am I excluded?" she asked.

Part II

Wednesday, 1 September – Friday, 3 December 1993

Autumn

Carpe Casus

6

Wednesday, 1 September 1993[9]

In the antique shop
Beneath centuries-old beams
Searching forgotten dreams.

    X replies…

> *In the dream's shadow*
> *An enchantment vehemens*
> *Animalis imaginatio.*[10]

---

[9] The couple had spent the vacation apart. There is no evidence that they communicated to each other during that summer break. They had agreed that their clandestine relation would have a rhythm dictated by the academic calendar.

[10] *Fragments*, p. 190.

Weep.

Tuesday, 14 September 1993

…Charlotte was a chocolate lover. She would weep for a chocolate. She herself accepted the label 'chocoholic'. An amorous perversion she even came to be proud of. One day she found herself out of chocolate, as was her companion. A real crisis. They were out of work, had no money and no food. She went to the local shop, went directly to the manager, made up a long story of woes and simply said, "I'm out of chocolate, please give me a job." The manager was touched, recognising the depth of the crisis. "I do need a workaholic, I've just sacked an alcoholic, and my wife is a sexaholic. But your companion has just been in," he said. He had made a quick decision, and had given him what he wanted: a part time job, paid in chocolate. "I'll never again have to weep over love and chocolate," said Charlotte.

7

X

…After the evening meal the campers sat round the log fire. One of the adults attempted to tell a story. It was halting, self-conscious and preposterous. Another adult tried but the result was no better. Out of the pack of small boys came a voice. "I have a story." It came from a boy identified by the adults as one who liked to keep himself somewhat apart. He came and sat near the fire and began his tale. As he talked, clearly and fluently, the image was set for a story about a strange medieval knight. The boy's eyes became animated and sparkled brilliantly and intensely in the light of the evening fire. Simply and lucidly the boy entranced his audience with a gothic tale of beauty and inner complexity about a Knight and his Lady. As it unravelled a situation of thrilling suspense was developed. The denouement was greeted with a collective sigh of pleasure followed by quiet conversation. In an atmosphere of quiet reverence the boy resumed his anonymity in the pack. A woman said quietly to her companion, "Therefore the moral of the story: in a romance we weep not for the loss but nobility and futility of love."

Rendezvous.

Tuesday, 21 September 1993

X begins...

> *...He heard someone coming towards him. It was a young woman carrying a pot. There was a pause and then she said in Arabic, "Moonlight dissolves the time of emotion. You are very late for the date with Laetitia and destiny. Come with me." He was surprised to learn of the rendezvous. He followed the woman into the caravanserai. "First you must eat and drink," she said and brought a simple meal, and while he was eating she began to tell dessert stories. He was tired, and then fell into a deep sleep. When he woke he was told both the woman and Laetitia had departed in a camel train across the desert. They had left a gift of several paper bags and a message: "Here is a poem in Arabic I have discovered – The Qasida. Please translate it into French. Here is a short extract: 'They who noblest live are those who make and keep their self-made laws. All other life is living death [...] a breath, a wind, a sound a voice, a tinkling of the camel-bell.'[11] Our next rendezvous will be equally unexpected." It was signed Laetitia*[12]

---

11   *The Kasida of Haji Abdul el Yezdi,* by R Burton (1880).

12   On 22 September X wrote a letter saying that through him she now had a lover, called Laetitia. X wrote: "I have had difficulty keeping this new relationship a secret, above all from my partner, who remains jealous and possessive. So I have joined a conjuration of secret lovers."

8

Acosmos replies…

…"Reading in three dimensions is an art I've tried to develop over many years," said the woman theologian at a Colloque in Ajaccio. "It's become somewhat easier for me in the last decade, after I left the desert, and with the proliferation of notions of fabulae, the unconscious of the text and so on," she continued. "One famous psychologist of course advised his students to do love letters," said a member of the audience. "I have always taken that advice to mean construct love letters." She paused. I then asked the theologian how she trained herself to visualise those letters. "Its become easier for me know that we are all used to seeing computer graphics in which objects in three dimensions, turn, rotate before your very eyes," she replied. "I personally have to exercise my imagination by seeing the letters not as the 'cross' section of a rectangle, or a plane through a cone, but as a rendezvous of two beams of light through a stained-glass window. I came to face words that are soothed on the turning shafts of light. I call my sacred visions written on light 'polka dots on moon beams' though of course my sermon on the subject of this new dimension has a more academic title: 'A mirage – not dialectical nor reformist love is transluminous'."

Karma.

Tuesday, 5 October 1993

…At the Coroner's Court, a report was read: "Brought up to conform, the boy rebelled. But the rebellion was to be of a new kind. Instead of an all-out attack on adult or bourgeois values, it would be more like a guerrilla war on the scale of very minor and insignificant infractions. He entered the world of action somewhere between culture and subculture. He called it his 'infract' in a kind of teenage skaz.[13] Of course, there are many different kinds of microtransgression. But, he reasoned, they basically fall into two different groups. There were those no one would normally notice and those which would always come to someone's attention. The first would in practice, for him, rarely if ever be the prelude to the second. This was, at least, his theory. Smoking underage was an example of the first if it was well concealed. The second involved two people clandestinely. […] It was by the discovery and systematic classification of differences between these small and apparently insignificant secret acts of defiance, the hearts 'problems' that he became the founder of the sociology of nano-deviance: the strange karma of disobedience quickly became a cult whose members including his cat lived for the moment and hysteron proteron."

---

13   A term coined by David Lodge (1992).

9

X

…It was once believed that the origin of meaning could be understood by interpreting the strange lines (called karma) which could be seen at the bottom of a translucent lake shaped like an eye. These lines could only be seen from high rocks overlooking the lake, and then only at certain times of the day in the summer months. After a time the ruling cult of readers became fearful that other members of the society might try to read the meaning of these lines. So they appointed from among themselves two specialist throwers to throw stones into the lake to create ripples. This would make the messages indecipherable. […] These two throwers, after a short time, were astonished to find that if they threw their stones in a certain way by skimming, new and more profound meanings could be read (they called nirvana). They kept these new revelations concealed, as they were instructed to do, from the new truths – you love me where I do not yet exist – as they encountered each other anew.

Palindrome.

Friday, 15 October 1993

…The man looked into the mirror on the wall. He could see all the usual features of his face. These did not interest him. He noticed that he could also see behind him a palindrome on the opposite wall. He peered closely into the mirror. Sure enough the outline he could see seemed to suggest four separate shapes rather like small portraits of animals found in the great cave paintings of Spain and southern France. One of them looked like a wild horse with a black flowing mane, another looked like a stupendous stag, the third was a shaggy mammoth. The fourth was an animal he couldn't identify: "That animal does need a shave," said his companion. "Through the admonition I am transported beyond poetry," he replied. "And I want to tell you about my new classification of haiku. Are you listening?" he queried. "First there are invocations, then evocations, convocations and provocations. I could explain each kind." His companion waited a moment and then said, "Surely you've missed out an important type: suffocations!"

10

X

...A man was happily married until he encountered another woman who was almost identical to his wife in all physical respects. At first the shock was considerable. After a while he became conscious of trying to identify all the minor differences between the two women. There was a slight difference in voice, a hint of an accent in the stranger whose secrets he still did not know. She was clearly attracted to him. At last the moment came when she engaged him in interlocution. He discovered her name was a palindrome of his wife's. [...] Eventually they discovered that their story making was also strangely inverted and transported. "You have turned my body and soul upside down," he admitted to the stranger. "But displacements are not realised in such tall stories," she reflected.

Representation.

Friday, 19 October 1993

…He said: "I drive by car to work each working day along a country route of great beauty. I've been taking the same route for many years and have come to notice that there is a bad accident black spot on the route. There have been many small and some serious collisions at that spot. I now take great care in approaching it. As I pass I try to identify the features of that conjunction which make it so lethal. It is not particularly undulating, not a place which invites the driver to take particular risks. The only feature which seems to be different is the very odd alignment of a tree, a huge rock, an old barn and beyond that an ancient sacred outline of a giant with a phallos and strange hands and feet (which didn't go with the rest of the body) in a field, a loved being in danger from puritans. As I passed this representation this morning I nearly shunted into the woman driver in front of me whose car and time had slowed down unexpectedly." […] "Had there been anything unusual?" "Yes, she had seen a group of people carrying a giant fig leaf."

11

X

Scene in a libretto for an opera:
…"What should be the representation of the ithyphallos in the postmodern age?" he sang. "It used to be a dagger or a sword, even a pistol." (The historian). "Today ithyphallic worship remains secreted in hidden cults among the gays, and the various porno cults of heterosexuals, and the phallists." (Sociologist.) "Perverse theories of course see the symbolic reflections of the phallus encountered on the body of the woman: in the sign language of rings, chains, bands, painted lines, even hair ribbons, but especially piercings." (Psychoanalyst.) "Simulations of the phallus have been made of wood, or bone or ivory, and of course more lately rubber and plastic." (Anthropologist.) "They arise in the Virtual now, a new form from the pharmacy." (Chemist.) But, "These identifications are imperfect, like the object in danger itself, and I speak as philosopher and curatrix."

Love.

Tuesday, 2 November 1993

X says…

…Two young women were comparing notes after making love with their respective boyfriends for the first time. "Ralph was very inexperienced, but sensitive," said one girl. "But it was all very physical and over very quickly as I expected. I'm sure he'll be better at it soon." The other girl hesitated. "Karl was much more experienced than I thought he would be." She looked up at the first girl. "I had to say no to things he wanted to do. I had to say no let's do that some other time and things like that. I thought I'm in love's wrong place." "So what kinds of things did he want to do?" asked the first girl. "Well it's a bit embarrassing, but he wanted to dance and run in the rain, to dip in the lake, and to play the flute in the moonlight." She paused. "Actually I had no idea what zeugma he was talking about it was so poetic so I cut the encounter short."

12

…The couple decided to tell stories at a unique address. She had noticed a traffic island at a busy road junction had become a beautiful garden of green grass, trees and bushes. It was tended with loving care by the gardeners each morning. One hot summer afternoon she led her lover across the busy road and disappeared into the private realm at the centre of the oasis. They exchanged stories to the continuous din of the traffic and heart beats, deaf to the sirens of the consumer society. They were worried when seen from a rare passing double-decker bus and they made a haiku and an exit. They were worried by the fact that they could not hope to seize their story by the tale.

Walled Garden.

Thursday, 4 November 1993

…She went for a walk with her lover, and on the inspiration of the moment they exchanged love stories in a clearing. It was late spring, and the sunlight filtered through the beech trees as they lay on the verdant mantle. […] Although they were bitten by ants and midges, it was an ecstatic moment of splendour in the grass. Should one continue? Time and love stood still in an hypnotic trance as they gazed deeply into each others' rich stories. Only later did they need the balm of love. […]

13

X

…One day, his muse saw him and beckoned to him to follow her through to a gate into a small walled garden. She shut the gate. "No one will come here," she said as she stood near him, adding, "but don't make any noises." Just as they whispered poetically someone passed. The couple became tense, tried not to move or make a sound, then relaxed as the footsteps faded. A little later, again, someone approached the gate and tried to open it. The woman tried to part from her partner but he held her increasingly tightly, in amorous time, and as she pronounced the psalm of love, he sighed in an ecstatic release of tension. The lock on the gate held, and the footsteps passed. The old man who used this short cut to his daughter's house muttered, knowingly, "Sounds like they are keeping some young beasts and orgasms in there now," as he reluctantly took another route.

Assonance.

Tuesday, 9 November 1993

…There is an undulating field. In the field there is a buttercup, a daisy, and some rare flowers. I could tell this was a field in which I was likely to find what I was looking for, a truly unusual orchid. I was right to search. I led my lover on. In the far corner of the field, over the brow of a slight rise, we could see the head of the rare solace we were looking for. But as we approached to the sound of a Mendelssohn overture, it moved and came towards me. It was Orchid the donkey: Ee Aw. And such a lovely Shakespearian Bottom. I praised this ass in a tale and strangely enough my lover says, "Like the Nietzschean ass, you say yes to everything."[14] […]

---

14 Barthes, *Fragments,* p. 177. Acosmos had further quoted at this point, "What is stupid is to be surprised. The story lover is constantly so," but this is crossed out.

14

X

...After the one night stand, the woman bathed, and then prepared breakfast for her lover. She felt good after a night of intense passion. The night had passed in darkness and she had not yet seen the ass of the man. She heard him stir. She went back to him: she led him to the bathroom where she bathed him. She washed him carefully, his body responded to her hands. "So this is what my subconscious has been lying against most of the night," she said. "No," said the man. "My body has become carnal. Last night it was pure soul, and now, through your attention to assonance, that soul has become a texture without memory," he said. "But the loved tale in the triune relation is de trop." She paused: "Soul and bacon?" she asked.

Library.

Friday, 19 November 1993

…The library was immense. From the plan at the entrance (or one of them) it was clear that there were many levels, linked buildings, book-lined corridors, several carrels, a basement of several interlinked tunnels, two or three specialist exhibitions. But as they went towards the light, to the top of the library where there was a small café, with a view across the city. He noticed the café was called *The Librarian's Revenge*. He took a look and was surprised to see a range of cakes in the style of famous books: bibles, novels, pamphlets, albums, diaries, a tapestry of illusions. They were made with great artistry. When he came to be served he chose a delightful little French tart called a 'Sartre'. "Can I give you something to go with it?" asked the server to the woman. "What have you got?" she asked. "Here you are, *La Nausée*."

15

X

…A woman said to her new lover, "I will not wear your ring but I will wear other items of jewellery or clothing for you." He thought about this and asked her to wear earrings. He would give her a number of pairs each of which would have a message for him when she wore them. If she wore any of them it would signify that she wanted to exchange stories with him. On top of this, certain earrings would mean either, that she would want a poem, or even a haiku. An unusual diamond-shaped pair would mean that he should compose one for her as soon as possible on seeing her, without exchanging any small talk, to transform it into an important event. She agreed willingly. One day, much later, they had arranged to meet for lunch in a busy mall and then go to the library. He suddenly noticed she was wearing the diamond-shaped earrings. Her eyes flashed with wit and anticipation. He took her to a lift and to the top open-air car park. It was raining slightly but they found a deserted corner near the noisy lift mechanism and hot air vents. "I submit I didn't know we would be able to carrel up here," she said, as he mumbled a bizarre haiku about Juliette and de Sade.

Object of Desire.

Friday, 3 December 1993

…She could see behind her in the rear mirror a car which drove up close trying to force her to go faster into the fog. The driver made angry signals for her to go faster, and then overtook. Another car drove up close behind, veered out and then cut in dangerously. Another car cut in narrowly missing her wing. As she was about to overtake a slow lorry it suddenly pulled out forcing her to brake savagely. This intensity, this struggle continued unrelentingly. She decided not to look any more into the rear mirror as another motorist made obscene gestures at her. She decided to stop. She went into the brightly lit restaurant of a service station for refreshment. She took her place in a queue. She thought she recognised the men from the battle on the motorway. The man behind her saw her drop her notebook – the cause of her desire. A man rushed to return it to its owner. Such a transformation, from egoism to altruism, resulted she reasoned from the prospect of immediate gratification of appetite and id. The man said, "Here is your Book of Dreams… did you know there are some people who never dream?" She didn't reply, but looked at him. "I am one of them," he said. "That must be rare," she muttered. "It's because I never sleep. It is rare; I'm studied by a university lab." She paused, and then asked, "What are the side effects of that?" "Well," he replied, "I'm deprived of the fictive life, I can't fantasise, and my world is the true world." He ate his meal and idiom alone. She abandoned her meal and drove off into the fog.

16

X

...His companion had something to say, he could tell. He was apprehensive. "I do have a lover – I mean another story lover," she said haltingly. "Tell me," he said. "My lover is called Laetitia, or 'Elle' for short – she is a young student in the faculty." After a pause, "I am bifabulant, as well as polyamorous," she said. "I want to tell you this because you will meet her, and, as many do, fall in love with her stories. There are quite a few squabbling over her." Astonished, he listened intently. "The rule is," she continued, "that you cannot encounter her, indeed hear her stories without my consent that is part of our contract." Another reflective pause and she continued, "If your id is attracted to her, that's OK[15] But your appetite for any story telling with her must be satisfied only through me." He nodded, wondering what sort of fictional future he had accepted if the other is divided.[16]

---

15 Acosmos had elaborated a theory of the id and the unconscious taking dreams as his focus. He argued that the existence of dreams reveal the human brain is wired to create stories without deliberation.

16 The following letters (slightly edited) were found in the archive:
December 15
Dear X,

I promised! [....]

I have been dreaming (of you). And of a '*discours amoureux*' (with you). It seems to me that RB does have things to say, but some good and some very strange. The lover's discourse is affirmative, and is expressive.

On the other hand, there is no reply, at least it seems so. Is this because he loves his solitude? Is this the reason for his suffering? Checking against the French I found the translation misses one of RB's haikus. (p. 132 Fr, 97 Eng.)

Ce matin d'été, beau temps sur le golfe,
Je suis resté longtemps à ma table,
Sans rien faire.

I hope you will find time to reply!
[….]
G

December 20
Dear G,

And I promised to reply. I daydreamed a lot about you. I was delighted to receive your thoughts […] In French one says *Je t'aime*, for I love you. Yet the word for love is *l'amour*, and lover is *l'amoureux*. I do want to be with you, so I'm suffering in the RB way. It is a declaration. In a sense it doesn't require an answer, it's not a question.
X

January 2
Dear X,

Thank you for your wonderful letter and I hope I am worthy of it. I'm only just getting to know you, and passing from acquaintance, to friend to story lover is exciting, there are different kinds of story and I'm suspicious of the romantic kind as you know. My feeling is that RB is trapped in a system of his own making, and what is interesting is that he has systematised it. Underneath his 'fragments' is a story of a relationship, and possibly the book is a long love letter to someone he refers to as X. He could have called it, don't you think, a '*vocabulaire amoureux*'? He invites other lovers to contribute to the project (Fr p 11; Eng p. 5). I'm making a list of possible 'figures' – but at the moment I think you are more gifted. What would you suggest?
[…]
G.

January 5
Dear G,

Your letter was again a delightful one. There is something in the RB comments on the wait, the anticipation, the feeling that something from the lover is coming, and whatever it is it will be unexpected, in the vein of the atopic. These ideas are appealing; they are real, true to me. But therefore I worry that if you do become fully known to me, something will fade – since it is in the excitement of the atopia that the story is generated.

There is something I meant to say, that does link with this. It is the fact that I am anon. Is it for you not only a convenience (our atopia is extra-marital and your wife is jealous of her contract) but in being secret it is its own private world. Didn't Simmel say something to that effect? But at the moment this clandestinity does suit me; you can trust me. I think perhaps you want this private cosmos so that in this story you can become someone you cannot be in your marriage. How do you feel about this?.
X.

January 7
Dear X,

Yes, for me you have become X. Let's not go into that in letters. I have to deal with whatever happens. We cannot become a couple in the recognised social sense. There is something in your notion of private cosmos, perhaps there is a 'figure' here – at least for us (but it was as you say in the essays of Simmel, Das Abenteuer, The Adventurer, 1911). All that is going to the serious, but there is in RB something of the comic. I was reading the figure of the 'embrace' – the 'motionless cradling' of lovers. Its here that 'we are enchanted… it is the moment for telling stories, the moment of the voice.' The complexity of the lovers' embrace as a site for fiction? For RB it is incestuous and then 'cut off' so the subject (RB) is doubled. (p. 105). RB is writing as a single man, gay, and his book is not that of an heterosexual encounter. I experienced this enchantment with you, but not the doubling (nothing more remote than the maternal.) I like the idea that in the

enchantment the voice appears, stories can be told, this is the micro-cosmos of the realm of make-believe. It raises a problem for me, since I have to admit that I love the atopia in you that you have made me believe. But I also trust in your own commitment to counter-transference.
G.

January 10
Dear G.,

RB's lover is a man, that is clear. Let's begin our exchange of stories again soon. I am preparing for some improvisations – let's start with '*attente*' – I am waiting for you. I have allowed my imagination to dream a little, and my dreams to come into my imagination. I also agree that we should write our own 'figures' in the style of Barthes. I have some notes on this already.

I should let you know that if it is only through L that you can really pass from pleasure to jouissance this might be the only way we can bring our stories to perfection. Then it would be a commitment to a special form of transference between us, the secret allusion.
X

Part III

12 January - 11 March 1994

Winter

Carpe Diem

17

Wednesday, 12 January 1994

What is it?
What it is.
Is it what?

X

It is what?
It's what is
What is id?

Viper.

Friday, 21 January 1994

X

...It was a hot sunny day. On vacation the couple walked through the lanes of a mediaeval Bastide village not far from the Mediterranean sea. Coming to the edge of the village near a patch of bare land a small snake tried to make its way along the lane but had become caught in the gutter. It was brilliantly marked. As the couple approached it reared up, and revealed tiny but deadly fangs in a strange encounter. "How beautiful it is," said the woman. The snake made an effort to get from the gutter to the grass, succeeded and was quickly lost to view. "That was an adder," said the man. "Its bite would have been lethal." "But it was so beautiful," she replied, "so perfectly reptilian. I didn't pick it up because it was so beautiful." She paused. "And did I pick up your challenge because it was seductive, as if a specific force impels my language toward the harm I may do to myself?"

18

…As the writer looked up he could see the passenger in the train was anxious to engage him in conversation. "Are you a writer?" she asked. "Yes. I'm a writer of short pieces of fiction," he said. "How do you do it?" said asked. "Well it's not really that easy to explain. I write mainly about people in exciting situations. And I have a theory I use as the basis of my technique of writing." "Well I'd really like to hear that!" said the woman. "Actually," he said, "it's quite complicated to start with. I have the view that each person can immediately be understood through something that is unique in their personal space, a fixed point – a void – which is attached to them and to which they relate all the time without noticing it. I've trained myself to pick up this point very rapidly. I then use this point as a key to the sketch of a situation or encounter." "That's most interesting," she said. "I'd like to know what constitutes *my* unique point of interest." "Actually, I have noted something about you. Your unique point of interest is just above your head. It's orbit has the shape of a perfect ring," he said. "Saint or angel?" "Ouroboros," he replied. She looked at him. "A viperous fallen demon of language that eats its own tale?" […]

Collecting.

Wednesday, 26 January 1994

X says,

> ...*I over heard a raging argument as I travelled by train once. The group of people down the carriage from me seemed to be pensioners going on an outing or holiday. They all began in good spirits. But then a dispute broke out concerning the term "hat". It was disputed that a "cap" or a "bonnet" was a hat. Someone else joined in with a definition of a "helmet"; another voice cited the "balaclava" and other types of helmet. Then a strong case was put forward to say that anything worn on the head was always a "hat" – this was quickly refuted by someone else who instanced a "hairpiece", someone else a "hood", someone else a "feather". Another voice joined the conversation to report they knew a relative who had owned a "Hat" shop. "It was clear," she said, "hats are only hats if you can put the word hat after them: 'trilby hat', 'top hat', 'straw hat'. A pause. Then a gentleman got up and with a suave gesture took off his hat walked up and down the carriage. "If you enjoyed the contretemps please be good enough to put your intolerable luxury into this cap. Subheading: I'm collecting for a good cause." "Chapeau!!" He took the cap and his leave.*

19

…In a town near a regional airport, two neighbours often talked across their garden wall. One was local and had rarely travelled beyond her region; the other was often away, travelling for many months of the year to destinations all over the globe. He said to his neighbour, "I'm never at home unless I'm away." He often described his trips and voyages in great detail to his neighbour, who said, "I'm never away unless I'm in my garden." "But I often think of you in your garden when I'm away," said the traveller. "I think of you as if in a far off country tending exotic plants." "But I mainly grow common plants and flowers, I don't do anything exotic or strange, except the odd impulse purchase," she said. "Don't you ever feel like experimenting with unusual plants?" asked the traveller. "Well I have been tempted by those new cannibalistic things; in fact I have a fabulous Venus trap in my special collection of them. But I keep these brilliant and rare things in a special place I call Huysmans."[17]

---

17 No doubt a reference to J-K. Huysmans' chapter 8 of his book *À Rebours* (1884), translated twice, once as *Against the Grain*, again as *Against Nature*.

Contrasts.

Friday, 4 February 1994

…When I used to visit art exhibitions with a friend she often didn't know whether to look at the paintings, the gallery visitors or the relation between the two. This particular gallery had a fascinating modern art exhibition. It was unfortunately full of school children looking at the pictures with their teachers. She passed a group of children in front of a painting by Matisse. "What is unusual about this painting?" asked the teacher. The children were full of bright answers but could not provide the answer the teacher was looking for. "Look," she said, "the face is green: it is a reflection of the wall colour." She walked on and found a group of adults looking at some paintings by Munch. The women looking at the paintings were very moved and some were in tears. In one painting called 'Jealousy' Munch had painted a woman between two men, one of whom had a green face. "Green with jealousy," said a woman. "No," said a man nearby clearly unmoved by this micro-fiction and who offered a contrasting view, "simply a reflection of the wall colour." She asks the question, "What the hell am I here for?" And I replied, "For the heart."

20

X

...The antique dealer went searching for old furniture around country farmhouses. He knocked on the door of an old farmhouse and as usual found himself among chickens, cats, ducks, and other poultry. An old woman came to the door, and then invited him to look in some ramshackle store rooms. "There's many a good cock come out of a tattered bag." she said. It was the first time he'd heard this antique expression and adopted it, using it frequently from then on. He was rather careless with it, and used it when he made passes at women who were generally alienated by his crudeness. His friends began to refer to his rustic, peasant and uncouth manners which contrasted so strikingly with his cultivated image of antique dealer. When he visited a remote fishing village and the door was opened by a beautiful young woman he didn't realise her jealous husband was watching when he said, in a crude attempt to seduce her, "There's many a good cock come out of these tattered bags." To which she replied, "Keep your own fish guts for your own sea maws." He turned and went off singing, "Hope has not died; it fled, unconquered, to the blue sky."

Shooting.

Friday, 11 February 1994

…It was a cold but clear morning; the sky was streaked with pastel pink and blue lines. The path led the man down to the lake by the old cemetery. A group of crows were calling to each other in a lonely tree in a field. A fox came into view and then disappeared into a hedgerow near a bird watcher's hide in the wood. […] The man then heard what appeared to be a furious argument, then, seconds later, a shot. The crowd of black crows lifted from the tree, ducks scattered into the lake. Then another shot rang out, just as the vixen casually walked across the track once again, tossed its head as if to say, 'he missed my exquisite point; he couldn't hit a bus'.

21

X

…The man was by profession a knife-thrower in a circus. He asked his lover to go onto the turning wheel while he threw daggers at her. His previous partner had left him. This was more than a job, it was a pure declaration of love he explained. The woman asked, "Why me?" "It's really a long story," he said. "I found by experience that I must be in love with the woman on the wheel or I am unable to throw my daggers." He paused. "I mean, throw my daggers without missing the target." Curious, the woman asked, "And what happened to your last lover?" "She decided," he said, "to try other risky occupations for greater financial rewards. These failed, so she threatened to leave me for another knife-thrower. I decided I would frighten her. I threw the performance of a lifetime. I severed several hairs of her body." He looked triumphant. "She will never perform that trick again with any one. She has now lost the will to take to the wheel." "What does she do now?" asked the woman. "She's in love with the man who fires the human canon and wants to become one of his projectiles, the first human dagger." "You think you can tease me by raising the spectre of the wheel," replied the woman. "Well now you're looking daggers," he said.

Circles.

Friday, 25 February 1994

After being found drunk with insomnia and vertiginous dialectic by his friend Huguette, he fell asleep…[18] When he woke up to subtle philosophical questions he became aware of the fragility of things, the transitory nature of forms, emotions, relations. […] In answer to her questions, he said: "There were various ways of thinking and reflecting on this pure panic of the world. One was to think of the world as a highway across undulating countryside. (Because the highway goes around the high ground however it is not at all clear what the ultimate direction is.) Another is to think of the path as passing in circles, spirals, and that as one journey ends another begins. There is a third possibility in which writing is always dense: perhaps there are two roads which intersect, one which is a highway that winds its way back into the future, the other is a spiral of paths which turn back in circles on itself." He fell asleep again counting the plot-lines.

---

18   J-L Borges, *Labyrinths*, 1970, p. 130.

22

X

...I decided to take the ferry from Dover to Calais, and took a comfortable seat in a lounge. Soon I sensed I was eavesdropping on an interesting conversation involving a skilled linguist. He was arguing with a woman that the very infrastructures of sentences were different for men and women. He was giving an account of his research. The account went into very great detail and complexity. He finished his general exposition and then went into the details of his research. This involved close analysis of various short stories given to him to test whether it was composed by a man or woman. It transpired – as it was pointed out by the woman – that what he had found was that every individual was unique and that was his major discovery. "No," said the man, "I couldn't claim that yet, since my results show that every time someone makes an utterance that utterance is unique to that individual." "And how do you interpret that finding?" she asked. "I conclude," he said, "that each individual is really many individuals." "And does that mean that each sex is really many different genders?" she asked. "I am both mother and father..." I couldn't hear the rest of his spiralling conversation from under the warning horn of the ferry suddenly announcing we were entering Calais and Soleil.

Subject and Object.

Wednesday, 2 March 1994

X

...I once encountered a couple who had met and become lovers because of the great skill and artistry of the man. He was a make-up artist. He met the actress while she was performing roles on the London stage, roles often requiring complicated work on her face. She realised that with this man her face, and particularly her nose, could be realised in virtually any form she liked. He also often philosophised on the meaning of "The Nose: Its Meaning In Life." Her nose was very small and hardly straight. But with a little effort and time the make-up artist could transform it into a charming snub, a sharp point, a daringly upturned hook, red, blue, or pink. The artist wanted to experiment on this woman and he had so charmed her with his artifices that anything seemed possible. At the high point of her career the Royal Performance arrived. "This is the high point of my career as well," said the make-up artist. He devised the most astonishing nose ever to be seen on the London stage (and that includes Cyrano's). It was long, beautiful, arrogant, yet fragile, many-hued. As the Monarch approached, however, so did a tickle in the nostrils of the actress. And as the Monarch came face to face an enormous sneeze shot the nose straight off into the large rose on the Monarch's breast. "Beautifully seductive aren't you," said the Monarch to the nose, "I am enchanted and bewitched."

23

…In the 1900s a little-known sect of theologians had noticed a significant change in the weather patterns. One minute it was hot, the next it was cold. The experience of day and night had changed imperceptibly as well, they seemed to oscillate more quickly. The theologians experienced this as a kind of "flickering" which others had simply soon taken for granted. […] These theologians talked of the new light. They worried about strange new pathologies of modernity, yet the medical profession could not identify them. "Then why are we seeing the world in a new way?" asked these theologians. After years of research it was conjectured that a number of new objects had appeared between the earth and the sun, objects oscillating at phenomenal and subliminal speed. The sect concluded that this was the "a-vide effect" as they termed it, (which others had wrongly dubbed "film") causing human relationships to go into an on-off mode, causing deranged intervals between story and its subject, and story and story.

Figments.

Friday, 4 March 1994

…My partner is a nurse and midwife: nurse to my longings and midwife to my ideas. I often lie in bed struck down by strange anxieties and fears. She cares for me. But then I go into a long pregnancy when she advises me antenatally on how to look after myself. If I feel bad about the situation I sometimes abort. I find the process of confinement and labour extremely protracted and painful. She stays with me, monitoring my body's transitions. She asks if I want a general anaesthetic or an epidural. My "children" come into the world at a violent and bloody crossroads, they are immediately sexed, washed and baptised. Most, however, I admit, are murdered in an act of savage infanticide by my partner who more and more suspects that they are plagiarised figments, and are thrown away with the bath water. My sadness belongs to that fringe of melancholy where the possible loss of the loved being remains inconsolable.

24

X

...I once encountered a man who was generous, open and welcoming. He worked in a large university department of literature and classical studies. But on one occasion I found him furtively folding some papers away on his desk as I entered his office. This happened on further occasions. I could see he was hiding a blue file. One day, by chance, I went into his office and while he went out briefly I overcame natural inhibitions and opened the file, called Carpe Librum. I found, to my amazement, forty or fifty sheets of paper with designs for book covers on them with his name as author. These were all phantom books about non-existent places. They had silly or fabulous titles, subtitles, drawings and mottos, even logos. They also had strange cover commendations written by well-known geographers praising the books for their bizarre and exotic achievements. Was it all a nonsense romance? His fictions remained pure figments and never did come to anything. "I assume this melancholy on the part of the other from which I shall not suffer," I said to myself, sotto voce.

Bounced.

Wednesday, 9 March 1994

…The post was particularly plentiful that morning. But among the letters was one marked "Return to Sender". And, sure enough, it had my name and address on the reverse side. It had been originally sent, by me, to an address in Scotland, to Charlotte Devon, in Banff. It had bounced back. Dejected, I realised that I'd sent my letter to Scotland instead of Charlotte Banff in Devon. On looking at the envelope more carefully I saw that it had been opened and re-sealed. Inside there was an explanatory note: "I opened this letter by mistake. I'm sorry. My name is Charlotte, and I accept all your explanations and apologies and fully forgive you. I am continually disturbed by intruders. If your Charlotte doesn't understand, write your story to me again." It was signed, sure enough, "Charlotte".

25

X

…He wondered whether he would be able to realise any of his many projects. He'd wanted to walk around the world, sail around the oceans, walk to the ends of the earth, and climb the highest peaks. But someone had already got there first. He'd set out each time in high hopes but he'd always got into difficulties, and never had enough will to persist to the end. One last great project might be possible, *he reflected. He researched the record books to find something truly magnificent that could still be attempted. He decided to perfect a gigantic trampoline: this would bounce him higher than anybody else had ever bounced. His aim, he announced, was "to go to the moon". The immense trampoline was constructed. The day arrived for his first "moon bounce". A beautiful day, the arc of the moon was clearly in view, and the moment had arrived for the realisation of a life's ambition. He bounced high, he was exhilarated. But he was passed, unexpectedly, by a woman 'skydiver' who called out apologetically, "Have we become non-Euclidean yet?" His jealousy was bitter and yet indeterminant.*

Personal Time.

Friday, 11 March 1994

…A couple had been together since childhood. They "married" in their teens, when he was 19 and she 16. At her birth he would have been 3, but of course when he reached 100 she was 97. The difference at 0 and 3 is only three years, and the difference at 97 and 100 is only three years. In relative terms, however, personal times are not straightforward. At her birth the difference is 100% but at 100 the difference is 3%. In effect, chronologically, she has caught up with him, has aged more rapidly. But in the numerical order she always remained the junior of the two and was always treated as a child. The other therefore aged more slowly, intractable, not to be found except in a very long story. […] But in another story, his companion grows young as he grows old.[19]

---

19 Lines from Blake, *The Mental Traveller*.

26

X

...Now would be a good moment to restructure our own time in terms of the occasions of each individual's life. All general, overarching times should really no longer play the role they once did. Instead of saying that the general strike took place in 1926, one should say it occurred when my father was 15. Instead of saying Margaret Thatcher was elected to power in 1979, one should say she came to power when my brother was 30. True, it might be thought this leads to an egocentrism, but in reality, it leads to fragmentation and dispersal as it did in the days of Herodotus. It would reestablish the importance of family, community and their personal rulers. My other would be defined solely by the time, suffering or pleasure he affords me. This is radical and postmodern, to contrast personal time against standard world time which is really an alien dimension. We didn't meet in 1993, when I encountered her I was XXX and Elle was XX.[20]

---

20 On 15 March X wrote a letter saying she was with Laetitia, at a conference at Oxford. She included a story, which seems without reply:

The drystone waller looked back over his work: a magnificent wall which he could see snaking its way across the rolling countryside of a great park. Each stone of the wall had been placed there by his own hands. At first he had thought of the wall as a human division: keeping humans inside or outside its limits. But as he continued he realised the wall was also colonised by all kinds of plants, birds, reptiles, animals. Against his formal instructions he constructed the wall with hidden chambers and corridors. He left small tunnels below the wall for animals to pass. In the spring he even built a nest and put a crystal egg in it to tempt a cuckoo. Sure enough, within a few weeks, another crystal egg had been laid in the nest.

Part IV [21]

12 May - 20 June 1994

Spring

Carpe Corpus

21 X wrote a long letter in early April from a Colloque she was attending in a Chateau near Caen in Northern France. The subject of the Colloque was the work and life of Michel Foucault (a decade after his death in 1984.) One day of the meeting was on the relation of Foucault and Barthes. X presented a discussion of Barthes and the work of Foucault on sexuality. Her long letter concerned in the main her meeting with two German academics, a married couple, Richard and Titia. Her letter reported that "Richard invited me to his room to discuss his ideas on fetishism in Barthes. I thought he was going to try to seduce me but no, it was to explain his ideas and the problems in his marriage, particularly their marital problem. Later I invited Richard to my room and as I was very attracted to him we began to make love but he broke off. He went into a long explanation about how he could only make love in a specific kind of narrative context. He said Titia would explain it. So later I met up with Titia to whom I was also immediately attracted to her striking beauty. She explained that she hoped I would come to their room after the evening meal for an erotic experience. I didn't reflect long on this as I was strongly attracted to both of them. Thus I was invited to join them. There was a lot of talking to begin with, and this was the narrative of their love story and with it the problem they encountered right from the beginning – which was that they found they could only 'bring their love to perfection' (my phrase) with a third person present in the love making. In effect, they explained I was invited as a fetish. I am looking forward to seeing you so that I can give you an account."
X.

Acosmos wrote a reply to this letter, but this has been lost. X wrote again to Acomos answering some of his questions and included a number of haikai that she had composed during the Colloque. "I have written a number of haikai, but the question which this raises is can a sequence of such short pieces which in themselves are not expressive, actually become expressive if placed in a chronological order? There was a discussion at the Colloque about the possibility of rearranging Barthes' figures so that they might accurately express his own story that is his own love affair."

Acosmos wrote a short reply: "For me the ultimate is the possibility that in love making itself the lovers exchange one haiku against another." To which X replied, "I like this suggestion but as I believe the couple have a zeugmatic relation the exchange should also be zeugmatic – so it would be more just if a haiku was exchanged for something else that would be raised to the value of a haiku. Or indeed less – perhaps it is Barthes who succeeds because his 'figure' is just affirmed to X who does not reply; is this not a zeugma? I would like to begin our next rendezvous with a haiku I have composed for you:
She looked away
And discovered
Time on her hands."

In the archive there is a dated haiku by Acosmos which appears to be a reply:
>He looked up
>And stumbled
>On an Idea.

Feminism.

Thursday, 12 May 1994

…"If you look out of the window across the park you will see that the deer are kept separate on one side of the field," said the guide. "We have here a good example of a ha-ha, that is a sunken barrier, sunken that is so the scene from the window is not spoilt by an ugly fence. This secret is not a deep one." This idea of the unseen barrier should have much greater currency a young philosopher in the visiting party thought to himself. […] He intervened later at the colloque[22] during a paper presented by a well-known feminist who had talked of a "glass ceiling". "Don't you mean a ha-ha?" he asked. The feminist walked over and hit him with her umbrella: "ha-ha" she expostulated breaking her exposition in the process.

---

22 Acosmos and X went to a Colloque in Bordeaux in May 1994. Elle was also there.

27

X

…"Certainly there is no God," said the atheist in a long exposition at the theological colloque. "But there used to be one, or rather, used to be many different Gods," said his feminist colleague in a very argumentative tone of voice. "It's certainly difficult to imagine living in a society with all kinds of Gods, and all kinds of cults associated with them," he said. "Did you know there was a cult of the Unknown God in one society?" she snapped back. "Was there a God of Humour?" he replied. "It seems that everything had to have its God, everything had its cult," reflected the atheist. "No," said the woman angrily, "they didn't have little cosmos (with its own time, its own logic) inhabited only 'by the two of us' – a cult of the narcissistic acosmic Story, as so many seem to advocate today!"

Finale.

Friday, 27 May 1994

The beautiful woman with jet-black shiny high-heeled shoes sang as she walked into the restaurant. All eyes left their sumptuous dinners to see who was singing. But just at that very moment a plump middle aged intellectual brandishing a revolver burst in. He was startled to find the classy woman and was stunned by her beauty and voice. She seized the moment and kicked the gun out of his hand. He'd perhaps mis-recognised her as a famous pop singer. With a flip she caught the gun with the heel of her shoe, flicked the gun back over her head into her hand and sang, sarcastically: "Over there, punkhead! Finale. No exits." She examined the gun. "Its defective, it doesn't work, the old instrument won't get you far: look." She pulled the trigger; out popped a small flag with the name of a rival restaurant on it. They both then turned to the astonished customers and took a bow.

28

X

…When I was young I went with my girlfriend to an organ concert given by Anton Zeiss. The organ was massive, expressive in appropriate hyperbolic proportions. He performed a remarkable piece in which one very high note was held for an inordinate time. As the piece continued it was, indeed, the only note played. It was a wonderful effect. After a few minutes, the organist himself appeared and talked to the organ while the note was still being played. Zeiss astonished the audience by saying the organ had developed a fault, one of the many pipes had now become permanently open. This produced a sumptuous continuous note. It was always a possibility with an old organ. I was disappointed with this explanation. Surely the organ had composed a unique finale, and should have been acknowledged just as the body speaks a non-verbal language, by imagining an extreme solution. "Yes," said my girlfriend in a phrase I will never forget, "I thought the organ would be a perfect baroque instrument but I found out it wasn't at all. It was pluperfect."

Veer Off.

Monday, 30 May 1994

….She moved so she could align the mirror of her hired touring car more accurately in order to see the rear image as she drove along. The image was a chimera, a fabulous creature, a combination of bear, a bird and a kangaroo, depending on how fast she was going. The shape was rather difficult to see and she strained closely to the mirror fearing that if she turned her head it would disappear altogether shattered by the slightest syntactical alteration. "You are becoming so vain these days," said her partner sitting in the back of the car as she suddenly veered off the narrow track into a different plot-line. "I have had a conversion moment," she said quietly. "To Hinduism."

29

X

...The composer talked to the woman while they were embracing. "Once I was a member of a jazz orchestra," he said. "I remember a particular occasion. The orchestra was playing a certain composition, but the rhythm was laboured, wooden, heavy. Suddenly the rhythm changed, the orchestra began to play with a quite infectious lilt. I looked up and could see the cause of the change – a famous jazz musician had come into the club and all the musicians in the band began to play in his rhythmic style." He looked into the eyes of the woman as his excitement mounted. "Your touch has changed. Which woman are you thinking about now?" she asked. "I resist making the other pass through musical syntax," he replied as he veered off the encounter in order to restore order.

Transgenic.

> Friday, 3 June 1994

X

*…They sat down to the meal. Expectantly, she saw from the menu hors d'oeuvres were to be served. Desire in the amorous state becomes something very special. There was a gasp as the cloche was raised to reveal just one large tomato. But the host quickly intervened to calm the mutters of disapproval ("*post-nouvelle *I suppose!") with the comment that this was no ordinary tomato. It was transgenic, hyperhybridic, irradiated and post-auric. The first 'fruitélan'. As she looked at the tomato it began to grow shoots for the two people at the table. The flowers were sublimely intricate, unfolding as though in time-lapse photography. As the tomato unfolded, a small plate-like disk formed on which could be seen a fabulous* salade gourmande. *"It even provides its own garlic," said the host. "But I can't persuade it to stop adding little slugs."*

30

She asked him to look into the future and he said, "...There will be a time when transgenetic research will make it possible for fruits and vegetables to exchange their shapes, tastes, perfumes, colours. The menu will change. Fruit will also be able to talk and express their own preferences in ways yet unknown of course. At first the fruit will experience exhilaration and enthusiasm. But after a while a great wave of sadness might come over the fruit and vegetables in the realisation that this was truly the twilight of the apple, of the orange, the passing of the aubergine. Fruit might become difficult to grow, to fertilise, to set. The Apocalypse of the Vegetable. Instead of books like *Animal Farm*, there will be bestsellers called *The Last Carrot*. Languor superimposes itself in this state of contradiction: this is the gentle fire. Other experiments try to find a solution, a new singularity not an apple that tastes like a carrot but a completely new transcendent fruit called a singularity-fruit. Small and remarkable it had one defect: it was found to be irresistible to a genetically modified insect that had reproduced explosively." She paused and said, "Shame about evil."

Disconnect.

Friday, 10 June 1994

....The young woman drank a quick glass of water, and looked at the scene. […] It was littered with the debris of the French massacre. A scene of total disorder and mayhem. Knives, bottles, lay at strange angles between heaps of rubbish. One could see stains of red exuding from the broken bodies and objects of this Napoleonic orgy. "Have you done the washing up yet?" came a sudden voice and lacerating phrase from on high. […] The two women began reflecting on the evening before: "That argument was ridiculous," said one, "especially to go to extremes and say the Bible was just a collection of pages and anecdotes." […] "And the reply that Wagner was just a miniaturist," said the other as they began to do the monumental clean up... […]

31

X

…Overheard in a bus queue: two women talking. "He has a very disconcerting habit. When you talk to him he very rarely looks you in the eye. He looks at something else: your ear, your collar, over your shoulder, your hair. Never your eyes." The other woman responded: "Yes, I've noticed this too when I met him. Its most unpleasant. It's shifty. You don't listen to him, to what he says. You don't trust him. He says 'He can't anchor his desire.'" The first woman replies: "I've been playing him at his own game. I never look at him now. I look into the distance. Either over his shoulder, or in a completely different direction. You don't listen to his stories at all then, you disconnect. But he does have a nice way of holding me tight and close. By the way, that's my bus and work coming."

The Meal.

Monday, 13 June 1994

X

Should I continue, go on composing poetic stories in the void she asked herself. "It's clear," she heard someone say, "that this table is just like any other table." Obviously she thought to herself the people at the next table in the hotel restaurant were engaged in deep philosophical debate. She became curious and strained to listen to the argument. She couldn't help glancing at the table in front of him, and at others. They all seemed to be made of the same material to the same design. She noticed the visible grain in the wood, and it could be aged. She also noticed that the tabletop had been fashioned out of a single piece and now formed a beautiful asymmetrical pattern. "Just as a tree is like any other tree," he heard someone say. "A woman is just like any other." At that moment the waiter arrived with the dessert: "The chef calls this 'essence of peach, essence of sun'." There was a pause, then, someone said, "One has to swallow the chef's poetic line, the sign of the times these days."

32

...A Chinese meal has to be eaten with chopsticks. Real chopsticks were fashioned by patient craftsmen, and were real works of art with an apparent grain. Now chopsticks are mass produced and presented at the table in wrappings. A storyline is stamped on each one, all different, sometimes humorous, and come in couplets. They can be separated from each other by a simple snap. After they are separated it takes skill to use them properly especially with rice dishes. But with other courses which have meat or rich sauces the sticks become very slippery and feel good in the mouth, their micro-stories consumed in the moment. They slide effortlessly down the throat, and join the rest of the meal later as a last sweet after tale.

Eclectic.

Monday, 20 June 1994

…The playwright sat at his table in a recently opened Mexican restaurant in the city. His page was empty, waiting for inspiration from his muse who was refusing to take part in the conversation. He wanted to write a play about Mexico, about passionate characters. The only thing that came into his head was "Peach Melba." He could not find any inspiration beyond this image. *What about the other characters?* he reflected. Surely one can't have "Knickerbocker Glory" in the same play? At that moment the waiter arrived, and he ordered a Peach Melba and a Knickerbocker Glory. He then wrote a quick eclectic outline of a play about the glorious sans culottes and Montezuma he called it 'Tempting Fate'. It could be the end of the affair he thought.

33

X

…Such was the force of the blast she was thrown back and almost lost consciousness. As she sat there she heard the sirens of the police and ambulance. But just as they approached they then began to fade again into the distance. They approached, and then receded again. This coming and going continued for a time, until the noises disappeared into the distance for good. Then she heard the sound of someone running towards her, the sound of many people running, sounds which peaked and then faded away. Suddenly it is another landscape. Everything went silent. "What do you think of my new eclectic composition?" asked the composer. "The promise of a new passionate encounter in silence is seductive," she replied, "I can feel it."

PART V

The Conference[23]

1 September - 9 September 1994
Carpe Hora

X

The lovers were happy. But she noticed at a certain moment there was an intimation of a slight imperfection in her love. This came to worry her when she had a dream about her lover. In this dream her lover's body became hideously distorted. She woke up in a sweat, and tried unsuccessfully to go back to sleep. She attempted to interpret her dream as she lay awake, but its meaning escaped her. She decided to fight it, not to accept it. Eventually she went back to sleep leading him by the nose into the cool grass on a summer's afternoon.

> The lovers took a holiday on a remote tropical island. They had a chalet in the groves near a silver bay. As they went to the translucent water to bathe they gathered coconuts. After bathing they drank coconut juice to quench their thirst. They made love and anointed their bodies with coconut juice. They decided to write stories on each other's body. The stories were instantly consumed. They became shorter and shorter. Finally they just said, "I love you," and then, "Love you," they just an, "o".

---

23 The conference on theology and art took place in Aix-en-Provence. At the time of this conference they exchanged stories, date and Kigo are missing;

…the episode of tenderness …can only be interrupted with laceration (Barthes, p. 225).[24]

---

24 This quotation was pinned to the first story. Attached also were two Haikai, but with no date or details.
    Frisson
    Fission
    Fissure

    Muse
    Recluse
    Meduse

Guardian.

Thursday, 1 September 1994

...As there was a Paris conference planned, it was agreed to take advantage to spend the time in a new experiment. "The idea would be to turn the occasion into an amorous and aesthetic adventure," he said. It would no longer be taking pleasure in various places of their choosing; it would mean placing the adventure into the event of the Paris visit itself he explained. "It would be," he said, "creating an aesthetic-chronotope: place and time beautifully unified.[25] For example, it would start on the very train journey to Paris... this journey itself would be an occasion when they could find or create an object of beauty..." [...] "It would need thought and planning and Elle would be the guardian and overlook the experiment: travelling to Donna Velata[26] a new kind of pilgrimage," she said. There followed a long discussion about the idea of making the self a work of art.[27] They agreed that their aim was to make their own relationship as a couple (and perhaps another) at certain moments, with an exchange of gifts, such a work of art.

---

25 Acosmos had read and written a notebook on M. M. Bakhtin's *Speech Genres and Other Essays* (1986) in which the idea of the chronotope is explored.
26 A statue of 1752 in the Louvre by Antonio Corradini.
27 Notably the writings of the French philosopher Michel Foucault.

34

X

…X and Elle met Zeugma at the Madrid conference as arranged, and they stayed at the same hotel. At their new style tryst he said, "Let's go back to the beginning and renew our adventure and its allure." "Elle can be my guardian angel." "I suggest we say our prayers first," he replied, "the prayers to Athena." "Lead the way," she said. She lay back to receive the holy allocation. She was surprised that he seemed to be struggling to get the words out. He searched his case and brought out a figurine and began a holy allocation in a strange tongue. "There is too much, you've become prolix." Elle was Medusa and amused. "I spoke in Greek to Athena to join our adventure to heaven and atopia, but my prayer was a bit muddled." "That's OK," said X, "I will join you in prayer." Elle watched the strange scene with alert fascination ab initio.

Homage.

Friday, 2 September 1994

X

...The story lovers and Elle met discretely at their Rome hotel location to re-establish their compatibility and to answer questions of further experimentation and theatricality.[28] After some preludes she said, "I trust you, please fulfil your fantasies, and don't feel inhibited. It's my gift in our pact of stories through Elle. Let's explore a new lovers' discourse as a dialogue. I think you will love the dangers it might promise," she said. "Now do use the right language in homage to beauty's raptures." As she knelt before him he talked of the beauty of her shoulders and superlatives. "I am your vassal," she said, "give me your oath and hand; I will give you a muse who will be beside myself." There was a short pause: "I won't forget this honour and moment," he said looking towards the muse. "Tell your story to Elle through me – if you can," she replied. His lips moved; she heard the nothing and the nadir.

---

28   A term developed by Barthes in the 1950s, *Critical Essays* 1972.

35

…"Let's work out our programme. Of course there are the sessions of the conference but we are going to the concert tonight – I have booked the tickets." In the evening they took their position in the promenader's gallery at the famous Albert Hall. There are no seats in the Gallery, the promenaders either walk or sit on the floor. […] Their plans were almost thwarted – there were too many people. They had to remain at the level of an amorous evening until Elle gave the signal that the coast was clear: holding each other closely to Messiaen's Sept Haikai, he asked X to join him to perform a short exquisite Haiku in the form of a figure through her. "Let my soul pass into yours." X at first felt this figure was transgressive; as she joined in the performance she became aware that she had become for a brief instant of ecstasy the vehicle for its energy and sublimity, a new transmigration He booked tickets for a private box for the next concert.

---

29 'The figure is a kind of opera aria' says Barthes, *Fragments*, p. 5; "my soul may pass into yours…" Diderot cited *Fragments*, p. 15.

New Lexicon.

Saturday, 3 September 1994

…The story lovers went to a French restaurant for lunch. There were many people, the best they could do to fulfil their new chronotope was to talk across the table. "There is a problem with the words, for example I don't like the word zeugma; but I do like syllepsis," she said. "We need a new lexicon," he said. "Let's list the words we like." They listed some beginning with the letter V and others. "But the aesthete's discourse is full of crudités. You have to eat a lot of the words and vinaigrette," he said. After the meal, going back to the hotel, he said, "It's getting late perhaps we should stop." […] "Take time with me," she said. "Then I will invite you to spend the night in with Elle and syllepsis in another world." As they walked he said he was beginning to feel unwell. He stopped, wretched and found a zeugma and crudités in the gutter.

36

X

...They were more successful that evening for the Ecstasy by Scriabin. They found a secluded corner for their own music making. After the concert they retired to their hotel for extended zeugmatism, "Pity to call it such an unpoetic name," she said. "Yes all those words people use are kinds of profane expostulations. I prefer the poetry sacred love and silence." "Well I like to walk, so we must find our own lexicon." They went for a late stroll in the city and came across a solitary figure, an elderly man wise and wizened. In a brief conversation he said he had been a lexographer and amanuensis but lost his employment for introducing fictional words into his work. "So you are looking for words?" he asked. "I am looking for my myth." They exchanged glances and etymologies. Then he said: "The important question in this meeting of the amorous and the sacred zone in ecstasy is that of the doctrine 'anatomy is destiny'." "What is the anatomy of the sacred realm?" they asked. "Yes, mu-koan," he replied ungrammatically and enigmatically. She understood.

Games.

Sunday, 4 September 1994

Two friends were discussing parallels between sport and love. "Let me philosophize," said one as they started their game. […] "…So there are certain erotic spheres (Weber), certain erotic zones (Freud) and certain amorous realms (Barthes). Just like the layers, troposphere, etc., and types of electrical wiring – red (live), blue (neutral), and green (the earth). But some of the colours used in competitive games are more complicated – take this game of snooker for example: you have the white ball which travels around to strike the colours – low colours (the green, brown and yellow) the medium, (the blue and the pink – placed just above the triangle of red balls below which is the highest value, the black. Clear symbolism: the blue spot is the navel of the game, but the highest value is not blue. It's a triune feast: two players as they take turns, and with destiny on the table, there is always a third party in the game." […] "Yes," said the woman, "but… in another game the chessboard is neutral but there are a lot of navels…"

37

X

...Thinking things over he wanted to clarify something. He began to talk to himself while adopting the strangely inflected voice of his Arab friend Sina.[30] He pronounced a monologue: Games intrigue me; there are many types of course. But what is interesting is the way of entering and engaging in competition, the exchanges, the various rituals. One is either inside or outside of the game when its in play, one enters not into the spirit of the game but into the activity (specific to each game.) It is an enchanted zone of engagement with an adversary. In an amorous encounter the lovers go into the enchanted zone. Are they then equal in this zone? No!! he thought to himself, it's a zeugma situation where a verb applies to two other objects but in different senses (OED), "She came in a flood of tears and a sedan chair" – to adapt the example. In the amorous sphere there are symbolic exchanges and a story emerges. But that's all it is he insisted, its zeugma not confusion of beings. His interior rhetorical encounter with himself over, he felt he had achieved something, as if he had made a decision and been victorious in his game.

---

30 Reference to Avicenna's famous Sufi thought experiment of the floating man, perhaps.

Legs.

Monday, 5 September 1994

…Two teenagers are tempted to try out the 'physical side' of their relation. Parents, friends, teachers, have made available all types of books, articles, pamphlets, drawings, photographs, as well as pre-coital counselling and clinics. Sociologists and psychologists have been invited to their college to give warning talks. Experts have demonstrated contraceptive devices. Vicars have addressed them on the moral issues, of the relation between the physical act and the "act of love" in a symbolic exchange. But there were no "image consultants" to warn the boy about the arousal he would experience on the way to the bedroom, or to prepare the girl for the uncontrollable laughter which would possess her on seeing his legs and huge embarrassment for the first time as it got caught in the tight elastic of his blue underwear.

38

X

They met at 10.00am,
10.15 in a park
Embracing in a dry ditch.

> *This yew is the right height*
> *Let's exchange*
> *Arms and legs.*

>> *Cars on the road.*
>> *A cool premonition passes*
>> *Caressed by apprehensions.*[31]

> *Heaven in a wild flower.*

---

31 Clear references to Hughes' poem *Lovesong* (1970) in this exchange, and then Blake.

Passion.

Tuesday, 6 September 1994

...In their box at the concert Elle drew the curtains and maintained surveillance. To the music Elle asked X, "What is kissing?" "Kissing is a fine art in itself. Kissing fashions have changed; it was once just the light pressing of the lips together. But now there is impatience about it. All the types should have poetic names – e.g. *The Fairy's Kiss* (Stravinsky) that the orchestra is playing now. There is the simple kiss on the hand in a symbolic gesture, to the kiss that passes from one to the other in the lovers' story exchanges – their passion and pneuma," said X. "But," he said, "in this piece the Fairy is the Ice Maiden whose kiss is a blessing and a curse: she kisses the heel of the baby boy and later by deception steals the place of his fiancée, places him under her magic powers with a fatal kiss and abducts him beyond time."[32] As X listened to the music she felt the music chill as though an icy wind had passed through it. She looked behind her and saw him with Elle standing frozen together... the metamorphosis of a metonym into a metalepsis... She recognised the lover's discourse.[33]

---

32 Acosmos and X found the pneuma in Agamben's account of mediaeval love in Stanzas (trans R. L. Martinez, 1993). In *The Fairy's Kiss* Stravinsky adapted a story by Hans Christian Andersen to frame a selection from the music of Tschaikovsky. Stravinsky said, "I only vaguely remember which music is Tschaikovsky's and which mine." Acosmos noted that Stravinsky speaks through Tschaikovsky, or it could be the reverse.

33 "...this declamation (frozen... removed from any praxis) is the lover's discourse", *Fragments*, p. 94.

39

X

... "Tonight," said X, "you may exchange stories again with Elle." He was surprised by the locution. "Elle has agreed to join us. She likes you, but of course the rule still applies and this is for all of us." In the evening X went to join Elle in her room and some time later returned with her. "I am ready for you," said X, so he led her by the hand, a brief embrace, and they started from small talk. Elle was wearing a light gown. He was immediately stunned by her beauty, the dark eyes under the trail of her long black hair. "You may only take her as your story lover allonymically through me and passion," said X, "as allegorical repletion." Then she said, "Bring your lips to hers so that your soul may pass into mine. Narayana."

---

34 The rule that X had laid down for their stories was that a direct love relation was prohibited between the other two unless a special exception was agreed in advance. Allegorical repletion was a concept developed in Camille Paglia's *Sexual Personae* (1991):'the term describes a redundant proliferation of homologous identities in a matrix of sexual ambiguity.' (p. 157).

Performance.

Wednesday, 7 September 1994

X

...She awoke from dreaming: was this dream a premonition? "I want you to indulge your pleasures," Laetitia had said. "I will oblige you, what would give you pleasure?" He reflected and said, "I want you to be my ghost writer at one of our meetings." "Why?" she asked. "Have you nostalgia for a particular occasion with one?" "No," he replied, "I've never had one, you would be my first and only one." So they fixed a date and specified certain phatic locutions, and the cost. "It will be then a short meeting, and will cost you a lot of money." So a place and time was agreed. And at the appointed time she arrived, entered and the door was locked behind her. She knelt on the prie-dieu *before him as agreed. The minutes passed. "I can't perform," she said, "please embrace me," as tears ran down her cheeks. "No," he said, "ghosts don't embrace; please talk to me quietly, ghost me the story." He gave her a considerable amount of cash and a seminal idea. Her story became spectral. As it unfolded it took on the character of a Hindu epic recounting the descent from the principle of evil of a wild flower of sublime beauty. She finished her story with a short stanza in Sanskrit, and without saying another word left the room and an avatar.*

40

…He spoke slowly, his eyes roaming as if he was gathering reflections recalling an unforgettable experience: "For some the mirror is essential in talking love, especially for the woman. First the mirror is essential for the woman to witness her own figure. Secondly it is essential for the woman if she is to see the act of expressing love itself, whereas it is much easier for the man And for certain locutions two mirrors are required for the woman." The voyeur watched her looking at the two mirrors, and a third person, as voyeuse, watched the performance: she could also be seen in a mirror before she passed through it. A sharp verbal movement by the *jouisseur* and a mirror fell and shattered trapping the voyeuse in a shard.

Pleasure.

Thursday, 8 September 1994

...As their relationship became more confident they began to play certain games that involved the invitation of others into the fantasy of the encounter. "Who do you want me to be?" he asked. "Imagine I am someone you are attracted to. Be unfaithful tonight with someone you are attracted to. Who will it be?" X thought and gave him a name of a colleague. "I find him very attractive," she said. So she began to have a relationship with his colleague, someone he guessed she would like to have a romance with. As they began and entered into this play her concentration was changed, it became more intense as she imagined her story for him. After a while she paused and suggested it was his turn. "Who would you like me to be?" He said he would like to play Elle. Again the encounter was different, the phrasing quite intense and the timbre of his voice had changed. He stopped, and said, "I have made a story for her, it was good, but through your presence the pleasure attained perfection." "I'm jealous – even though you have not broken our precepts," she said.

41

X

…"I think we should have much stricter rules," she said. "Yes let's think about it," he replied. They drew up a number of rules, some strange, others bizarre for their next encounter. Rules for the construction of stories as they became more elaborate. They would have to include quotes, references, and a kigo word (the same in both stories). This kigo word would have to be unusual in itself not commonly occurring in the discourse of pleasure. There were to be new rules of how they prepared for and engaged in practices of story telling – such as the preparation of instructions given in advance by letter. And in the encounter the menu of the exchange itself. All this was to no avail: all the rules were broken to their immense concern and jouissance in the exchange.

Falsification.

Friday, 9 September 1994.

…She has asked him, "Who dressed the two dolls ready for the carnival?" So he pronounced his doctrine: "The end of romantic love and the beginning of acosmic love," he said. "They are two fundamentally different kinds of love and I abandoned them to the brocante market. The romantic one idolises the other into a loved being reflecting his/her desires of the imaginary other. The ascosmic one delays the onset of love (if it arrives) as the real other is revealed in the encounters – love grows. Thus one can fall in love and gradually have illusions shattered, or start without illusions and fall in love with a real person." "But," she interjects; "can the two be combined? Isn't that the ultimate? This would be when your 'illusions' are gradually found to be valid, and the process is one of validation of an hypothesis." But he said as ventriloquist, hypotheses are never finally validated. One should use the method of falsification pressed to the limit, the love story is always a faith in doubt, not a belief not a truth, in suspension over an abyss. Love, the sartor, came as illusion and fetish.[35] "They did not want to be abandoned."

---

35 "Whatever", Agamben, G. (1993).

42

X

...She said, "I want you to send me another letter in advance for the next session. I was disappointed with the last one; I feel you are not pressing your acosmic love as far as you can." So he wrote a letter which surprised and frightened her. She was instructed to go to one of the city's dream shops and buy some items. The instructions were detailed. Just before the end of the session he used alliteration with her for the first time. Then he gave her a syllepsis and further instructions. She followed them: "I love your potency," she said. Just before the end of their session, he said to her, "Now it's your turn." They embraced and suddenly she felt her arm and then her whole being disappear through his smooth skin, into his body, into the viscera – but instead of finding vital organs there were phantoms, dreams, memories, desires and nightmares. On her reappearance she was in a flood of tears and falsifications. She began to arrange a veil of falsifications over her head and body; she stood in a frozen posture, became marble, Donna Velata.[36]

---

36 A story exchange of indeterminant date occurred about this time

> X. *Their walk took refuge in a disused tunnel. Through their embrace they received each other's warmth. He became more feminine, became Clothilde, to the attention of love. Their embraces passed from holding to enfolding. The tunnel became a chamber of strange echoes. They listened to each other, sensing intensely the rhythm of their breathing. Then as Elle she taught him to receive her breathing; to make his life depended on her. For a moment*

he expired; then again she breathed life into him. Suddenly from out of the darkness a tramp passed: "Tunnel of luv," he muttered; "there are two other couples further in and their stories get darker."

> She becomes masculine, becomes aroused,
> she expresses love in joy. Suddenly she leaves
> the tight confines of the vehicle and goes into
> the cold rain. He joins her against a green
> oak. In wild abandon they hold each other's
> attention passionately and fall into the biotope.
> In the mud they loose track of place and time.
> Gradually she leads him back to the vehicle…

A letter from X dated 10 September says that she wanted 'to continue only in a relation of the duo of story lovers. Elle is dead'.

Part VI

14 September – 9 December 1994[37]

Autumn and Winter

Carpe Nihil

---

[37] An exchange took place in the week beginning 13 September but not dated or detailed:

The last leaves turn
Sensing the void
Nothing without end.

                X

                          The skies darken
                          Even time slows
                          A plagal cadence.

X
He went into the woods for a walk alone. By chance he came across the very spot where they had bathed earlier in the summer. He went towards the spot as an elephant walks towards the carcass of a dead member of its own species, with dread and reverence. He sought a trace of that encounter, proof that it had been real. He couldn't find one, not even the slightest indentation in the grass, or trace of chewing gum that he had flicked out of his mouth before they had entered the water...

            H_20 is the well-known chemical formula for water.
            Water is composed of two gases said the professor,
            as they combine they seem to get heavy and
            condense (not to be confused with 'heavy water'

of course). But, added the student, something has happened to water and its formula, it gets longer as history proceeds. There are now not only hydrogen and oxygen atoms to take into account but many more chemicals as the years pass. One now has to look for H_2O in a pure envelope, a niche, somewhere where it's more than just ordinary water: a plastic bottle on a supermarket shelf.

43

Tuesday, 14 September 1994

A strange hand draws
Love's imperfection
In life's solitude.

X

Estar en tinieblas[38]
An incomplete effect
Life mysteriously realigned.

38　*Fragments*, p. 171.

Clues.

Wednesday, 21 September 1994

…The woman's body was found in the train's first-class compartment slouched on the seat with a strange arrow through the heart. The arrow had a note on it. 'The night of non-meaning'. It was virtually indecipherable, full of strange and exotic symbols unknown to the police investigators. It was sent to the University for expert analysis. The linguistics expert was soon of very great help to the police. He showed that the message read "I deserved death". The body carried many clues: other pieces of esoteric literature which the expert interpreted as bonsai stories. They were strange stories which he saw as parts of a larger design. He reported quite frankly, "Yes she had indeed deserved to die, the fiction itself constituted sufficient ground." The police seemed convinced in the absence of evidence to the contrary.

44

X

...It was apparent to the police that the victim had suffered a lingering death, and that crucial parts of the body were missing – the tip of her nose, ear lobes. "The murderer seems to have been systematic and left us many important clues," said the detective. "But what was the cause of death?" asked the assistant, "for all these wounds are relatively minor and would not have been fatal." "That's the mystery," said the detective, "she seems to have died of shock." On further investigation new facts emerged. "It seems that we have found some pages of a horror story ('The darkness is transluminous') on her, apparently written by her companion. Some believe this was the cause of death," said another assistant, "the people who have read it are all in a state of shock." "Let's hope its machine readable," said the police.

Words.

Friday, 23 September 1994[39]

…The man always liked to play the role of Father Christmas. He did this in many department stores, and especially liked to take up his residence in a grotto. He owned his red robes, white beard. He was sometimes hired for private parties. He performed for relatives. He loved being the bearer of gifts. But falling out of love he decided he would kill off his lover in a unique way, through kindness. Thus she became increasingly pampered and spoilt. […] His presents were excessively sweet, sugary, fatty, yet completely irresistible engendering joy. At Christmas he presented her with a box of chocolates. On each chocolate was the word of a story and they had to be eaten in a certain order to reach the story's climax. But he didn't reckon on the fact that she had become so greedy that she would down the fictional poison in one go, so she never experienced the slow ecstasy he had composed for her.

---

39 An exchange of Haikai took place dated simply September 1994.

>Frisson
>Fission
>Fissure

X

>*Muse*
>*Recluse*
>*Meduse*

45

X
…She was clearly very excited. "I've got some news for you," she said opening the parcel he was carrying. "It's a completely different, revolutionary type of book which I bought in a London antique shop as a gift." "Well that's something," said her partner. "Let's have a look." She took out a circular object and several disks. "In this system," he explained, "the eye stands still on the page on a single point, but the book revolves at a speed determined from a range by the reader." He indicated the speed adjustment mechanism. "The point is that only after a certain speed do the really special effects of reading at high velocity begin to happen. Why don't you try the 'gyrotext'?" "Yes, give me a disk," she replied. "Some of these disks have not been read for many years, try this one." It was called 'From Prose to Poetry'. Sure enough the text appeared and as she fixed her eyes on a specified point she could see the idea of reading it this way. Then she moved up through the gears to high speed, and could see that although the words still formed the basis of the text a completely different rainbow effect began to be visible. She became completely captivated as the higher form of the poetic vision appeared. "They are very short, but ecstatic," said the man. "Yes," she replied, "rather like a brief rainbow that lasts a second or two." Then she felt the brilliant old story teller simply disintegrate in her hands. The world became sensuously impoverished, abstract, erased.

On the Other Side.

Wednesday, 28 September 1994

X

...The writer of thrillers, mysteries and crime fiction decided to create a whole new genre of crime stories. These would be short, very short flash texts but so complete they would astonish. After reading them other stories and tales would always seem so long and redundant that the texts would gradually fade from the canon. One of the first mico-fictions suggested that X killed Y. But in fact Y was not dead, recovered to haunt X. After a time, however, Y was declared "missing presumed dead". But as time went on X was horrified by the number of signs of Y's reappearance. She contacted the police, but their investigations came to nothing. The woman sought help from alternative medicine after developing a range of nervous symptoms. The one source of real help was a psychic healer who said, "Your fictions are simply less deadly than those of the ghost writers on the other side." So the case was eventually resolved by seducing the ghost to an old cow shed such that it exposes itself without protection, and killing it savagely within a glorious paragraph.

46

…Two climbers, unbeknown to each other, ascend a mountain from different sides at the same time; and as they reach the last few steps they see each other and make a mad dash for the summit: they each carry their national flag, which they implant not on the peak but on each other before falling to their respective deaths in the territory of the other; and had they fallen back into their own territories war would have been certain. The fallen bodies were unable to reach any grandeur, said an ex parte report.

Phantoms.

Monday, 3 October 1994

...The dead woman was killed by a sword. "A very unusual sword," said the detective to his junior partner. "This wound is undoubtedly the key fact of the case. If we can unravel its meaning we will solve the case," he said. The sword had been left in the body. It had entered just below the ribs and exited horizontally near the spine. It was an unusual with many features commonly associated with pens and there had been sheets of blotting paper lying near the body. They had been used to mop up blood. "I think we are looking for a writer," said the detective. "Yes," he said, "the bloody evidence is pointing in that direction. Perhaps someone is trying to demonstrate that the pen is mightier than the sword." All the possible variations of motive were calculated, including the possibility that she had accidentally (or not) fallen on her own sword. But the junior detective suddenly resolved the mystery by a visit to the fencing club at the nearby university. He discovered a fencer who informed him about two writers, a man and a woman, who regularly duelled with rare sabres shaped like oriental pens. The duellist was arrested and falsely confessed to killing his lover. *I produce a myth of grief, and henceforth I adjust myself to it,* he thought to himself. He loved his own phantoms, which always included his lover and a murder.

47

X

…The man was conspicuous with two large daggers in his belt crossed in the shape of the chiasmus, the X, the sign of mirrored inversion. One of them had blood on it. But at the fancy dress party of the club no one took much notice. He wore a black mask. No one cared who he was since he danced and duelled so well. It was only later during the police investigation that the identity of this man became of supreme importance. A woman he duelled with commented on his daggers and on the blood, and how difficult it had been to remove it from her dress. "My grief is not an illusion," she insisted. The police called him the Phantom Two Daggers when they arrested the woman for the "suicide" of her lover.

Boy.

Friday, 28 October 1994

X

…"I am poor but I see you are rich," said the beggar to the young boy carrying a bright new shiny bag with the logo "Ultra-Adhesive Tape" printed on it. "I need this tape," said the boy, "to repair my atlas." "But Atlas, the God who holds up the sky, is already old, and very infirm and has abandoned us. Can Ultra tape regenerate him?" asked the beggar. "I do not have the wealth to buy that kind of tape," replied the boy. "Anyway the old man that used to sell that tape moved somewhere else some years ago." "No, like me he took to the streets," said the beggar. "Since then he died, and many people have begun to notice that the charts, maps, city plans, have become fragile, liable to tear easily, and there is no remedy. Now the world has become a village, there perhaps is no longer any need for new maps of the globe, only a need for a new God called Atlas. There exists a higher value for me," said the beggar to the boy.

48

…A woman finds that a robin befriends her in the garden one winter. She feeds it regularly and it sometimes flies into her kitchen. […] One day it suddenly disappears. *Maybe it has been killed by a cat or a magpie*, she thinks. "No," says the small boy from next door, "I saw it away in the woods by the lake. It said it was simultaneously loved and abandoned." […]

The Writer.

Wednesday, 9 November 1994

…The writer sits at his desk. His paper is blank. It is not that he is unable to think but he is reluctant to write down what comes into his mind. He goes to the window just as an exotic bird alights on a branch and begins to sing a less than enchanting song. "Do you sing from memory," asks the writer. "Yes," says the bird, "my mother sang the same song." "Why do you sing the same song?" asked the writer. "You have misunderstood," said the bird. "All my songs are new, I sing from memory, in homage to my origin to which I return each time." Then the bird said, "In a world that is changing I imagine myself dying without leaving regrets behind." "Is that possible?" asked the writer as the bird vanished from view.

49

X

…The writer sat down to write. But on this day he was not in the mood for writing. He was not inspired. On the blank sheet of paper the figure of death passed. "But I must write," he said. "I am a writer." He looked out of the window and saw a nightingale alight on a branch. It began to sing a long and beautiful song. "Why do you sing so beautifully?" asked the writer. "If I do not return to sing," replied the bird, "the sun will not rise, the spring rain will not fall, the grass will not grow, and there will be nothing for you to write about. And death will not be distracted." That thought the writer is the delirious assumption of dependence as his mood changed and inspiration returned…[40]

---

40 X has adapted a story by Hans Christian Andersen used by Stravinsky in his ballet *Song of the Nightingale*.

A Last Exchange.

Friday, 18 November 1994[41]

…The writer at dusk that winter night again was faced with a blank sheet. A brilliant white owl flew silently through the open window. "I have changed," said the great owl. It flew onto the writer's outstretched hand. "I have learnt to survive in the world. My sign is chiasmus, I knew Minerva. Perhaps we will meet again when you will be better prepared for me. We will perhaps then exchange our desires, fears, love and wisdom. You take inspiration from the birds because you see them as wonderfully free to fly away. But you lack the wings to fly: watch…" And the owl flew away. Starting from a negligible trifle, a whole story of memory and death begins and sweeps me away said the writer to himself. The owl looking back said, "A cage goes in search of a bird."[42]

---

41 X wrote a story in this week:
As the train neared its destination I noticed the heap of luggage piled up by the door of the carriage. Cases of all kinds, colours, shapes, designs. One particular case took my attention. It was asymmetrical with a bulbous end. It had a number of zipped pockets and some strange symbols printed over one end. As I made my way out of the train compartment I saw by chance that the words were "bone idol". Curious about what was in the case and the symbolism, I watched as the case was picked up by a tall man who found it quite a weight to carry. He was smartly dressed and had a serious air about him. "Do you mind if I ask you what's in this case, it has such an odd shape?" I asked as he descended from the carriage. "No not at all," he replied. "Sartor Resartus. It's my musical instrument in this case."

42 An aphorism from Kafka (Zurau).

50

X

…A couple took their seats in the train opposite one another next to a window. They seemed to be in the very last stages of an acquaintance. They began to exchange confidences, and to talk about expressions like "eye contact", "making first contact", "contact lenses". The conversation moved on to consider the possibility of the eye as a source of pleasure. The man said he often noticed only painful sensations like bright light from the sun, or strong beams. "Yes," said the woman, "I experience this but I also experience pure sadness through the eyes. It could be a soothing light, a particular colour, moonlight, a rainbow." She said, "I'm sure to know when this happens as slight tears will form; we are coming to the station where I get off; let me look into your eyes once more; the light is changing fast; and now through my bitter tears you already belong to my memory." On his own he said in a low voice, "I am afraid of my own dissolution."

The Ending

2 December – 9 December

De te fabula narratur

51

Friday, 2 December 1994

Disjecta membra

Haiku I
As far as Samarra[43]
Affectless tears scatter
My annihilation

X

Haiku II
Sudden fears scatter
Sibylline fragments
Estar a oscuras[44]

---

43 Allusion to a story by Somerset Maugham included in his 1933 play *Sheppey*. Acosmos wrote and then deleted his own version of this story.

A group of haiku writers met regularly. One of the most distinguished was surprised one day to catch a glimpse of death on a street corner looking in his direction with interest. He informed his fellow writers he would have to miss the next meeting as he had to catch a flight to Samarra. Death, on hearing this, said he was surprised as he had an appointment with him and a haiku on the morrow in Samarra.

44 *Fragments*, p. 171. The kigo word, 'scatter' alludes to Agamben's "the communication of singularities… does not unite them in essence, but scatters them in existence." *The Coming Community*, p. 19.

Death.

Friday, 9 December 1994

Obituary

...Giorgio Acosmos died in 1995 of natural causes. He was educated at number of universities (Cambridge, Paris, Zoa), but life itself was his University. He published two early monographs: *Theatrical Improvisations* (1965) and *Memory, the Unconscious and the Cadenza* (1968). He worked for many years as a scientist at the University of London. He was a distinguished theoretician, and discovered important universal qualities of fading light. He formed a late interest in language and in the importance of theoretical fiction. His main life project was to attempt to put into practice the reversal of time. It was the final point not the first which was for him decisive, and each moment was internally divided into two purely coincidental points, matter and antimatter. He tried to demonstrate this in his life. All his close relationships were always founded on opening and closing, the latter being the key to the reversal of the former. Strophe and anti-strophe, gift and counter-gift. But the difference between the two became a theoretical problem, for in order to reverse their significance, one has to know, he argued what this difference was. This led him to research into the *Haiku*, which formed the key to his last discoveries. He became afflicted with zeugmatism. His death took the form of a *Haiku*. He went fishing and caught a carpe noctem and pneumonia. A tall thin taciturn clergyman attended his funeral.

52

X

...He became somewhat eccentric, walking often to his appointed grave which he had bought at some cost. The basic problems of western culture stemmed from its abandonment of the certainty of the time and place of death. As he grew older, he realised that he would still be in the full vigour of life when his appointed date of death had been specified. He became depressed, melancholic and ill. On the day of his appointed rendezvous with death he went with the ghost of Laetitia to the cemetery in Samarra, having already placed obituaries in significant papers and settled all his existing debts. A violent thunder storm broke just as he reached the grave site. As he bent over the grave a lightning bolt struck the yew tree where he had made love a few yards away, and killed the ghost of Laetitia Gaudium ("L"). First he reasoned that Death had simply missed His target. But then he concluded God had granted him a second life. Death itself is not a haiku he said in his inaugural resurrection lecture. The true end is always a successful transition through poetic justice. His (ex-) story lover continued to haikai with him

occasionally from another place, but no encounters or dialogue.[45] *She regretted he had lost his "Elle" and sense of zeugma.*

---

[45] 'One of those close (the adjective is excessive) English friendships that begin by excluding confidences and very soon dispense with dialogue…[to] carry out an exchange of books [and haiku]' (Borges, *Labyrinths*, p. 30.); a note appended here by X.

53

Coda

They exchanged many haikai between 1995 and 2002. On Friday 15 February 2002 they exchanged the final haikai.[46]

X

> *Memories persist*
> *Chronos topos eros*
> *You are in me still*

> To find you again
> From time to time
> And then the story lets go

---

46 Acosmos died in 2014 aged 91. I contacted X about his manuscripts and asked her some questions. It transpired that there was a considerable age difference between them, she was born in May 1968.

X wanted the following as epitaphs

"We were friends and have become estranged… and perhaps we shall never see each other again; perhaps we shall meet again but fail to recognise each other…" (Nietzsche, cited by Barthes, pp. 222-3).

"All things have their time." (Zahnarzt de Giorgio).

The lover desires the loved story with all of its predicates, its being such as it is […] this is the story lover's particular fetishism. (Agamben, 2, p. 2, translation modified and adapted.)

Addendum

A Short Note on the Storytelling

I had a conversation with X, December 2014; she was then Reader in French Literature in London. I asked her to tell me about the stories. She said, "I was attracted to Giorgio – I never called him anything else – to his wit, humour, erudition, inventiveness. We prepared for the story exchange and this took a lot of work. We chose the concept or 'figure' as we read Barthes, and from this we each had to choose a phrase to insert into the story. The model for this was Pierre Menard, the famous figure in Borges' short story.[47] He chose the Kigo word and this word had to be used in each story of the exchange. But as he very largely began the exchanges from his prepared idea I had a much more difficult task to reply in a certain improvised way in the exchange. My stories were about encounters, his were more abstract. He had good memory, but I was gifted as well with an excellent memory and gift for playing with stories lines and quotations." I asked about the exchange itself. She said, "It was always a rendezvous. Often on the train going to or from work. But other occasions as well, such as over a meal, going for a walk. It was always in good humour. The moment of storytelling was one of vertigo…" And the record? She said, "He made notes, wrote it up, and I added my corrections from memory and from notes I had made. I have edited them slightly for you. It was all first of all 'in the head' as a specific form of 'sensuous involvement'[48] but it ended up being on paper." Any final comment or reflection? "I loved it. It was great fun. I was attracted to him, but he insisted on keeping

---

47   J-L Borges, *Labyrinths* (1970, pp. 62-73).

everything in the fiction. He said the stories desired each other as poioumena. I know he kept a diary, as I once saw it, read bits of it. It was quite revealing as he put in a lot about me and the occasions of story telling, each poioumenon. For example he noted what I was wearing, what time it was, the weather, my hair do, things that would remind him of the event itself, bits of conversation, his own thoughts and fantasies. It also had what he was reading that might be relevant, lots of short quotes. At that time it was all about Roland Barthes in English and in French. Giorgio was the one who opened it all up for me, the theory and the practice: we were 'story lovers'." There are strong hints that you had an affair with Acosmos, was that the case? "I certainly pushed him in the stories in that direction, especially when we went to the conference in Aix-en-Provence we spent a lot of time together; the real affair, as it was for me, was with Elle in the stories [...][49] I think of these affairs as neo-platonic in which I was a prosopopoeia, in September '94." I pressed again for more information, and she said, "I can tell you he saw Elle as metonym, and even as meta-lepsis; she was not completely independent, yet semi-detached from me; became sacer, she was for him a fetish and who died savagely and suddenly. He never forgave me for this. Our relationship went from an aesthetic to a moral crisis over this."

Although these interviews were convincing there was a remaining doubt in my mind. I decided to try to find corroborating evidence. I decided to contact one or two people in his Department of the 1990s. Eventually I found someone would was described as a close friend of Acosmos. I told him what I knew. He said that I was right to want more evidence. As regards X and Elle he said, they were X's two sisters who became academics in their own right. They knew about the stories and they kept up the pretence of the exchanges as real ones. But the reality was that the stories were written up after the strange death of X in 1991, it was a kind of therapy for him. So he did have a passionate affair with her but it ended when she was killed by a lightning bolt while on holiday in India. As their relationship was secret, he could not mourn her publicly, only to me. The story exchange idea was to bring her back to life.

Again I was not completely convinced by this. I searched for another witness. I made a much more thorough search of Acosmos's library and archives. Eventually I found a bag, and this contained small notebooks. This turned out to be the lost diaries for the 1990s. There was not death by lightning strike. The dairies confirmed the existence of X as a story exchanger, but even her identity remained concealed as X. Their meetings were recorded and selective details were entered: she was wearing this, her hair was arranged thus, she made this or that remark. And to my surprise there were one or two short paragraphs in a different hand, indeed X's own hand it seemed. She had read their pacts, commented on them and initialled them. There are many references to X's skill as a story improviser, and one long and detailed analysis of a particular story by X (7 September, 1994) which he noted was a turning point. It was clear that the stories exchanged at the conference were very consciously different in construction and included X, Elle and Acosmos in them as trio sublimations of the real exchanges of that time and place between the two of them: Elle was a fiction in the fiction but also a character in the drama of their relationship.

The story told by the retired academic was simply a cover story, unless the dairies themselves were pure fiction. The weight of evidence of the dairies, however, seems conclusive.

Bibliography

Found in Acosmos's collection for 1993-5 in a large paper bag with the manuscript such as it was, and letters. A second bag with diaries 1993-4, 1994-5, with some pages missing apparently simply torn out.

Agamben, G., [1] 1993. Whatever. Ch 1, in *The Coming Community*. Translated by Michael Hardt. University of Minnesota Press, Minneapolis.

Agamben, G., [2] 1993. The Theory of the Phantasm in the Love Poetry of the Duecento. Translated by Ronald L. Martinez. From Stanzas. University of Minnesota Press, Minneapolis.

Barthes, Roland. 1975. *The Pleasure of the Text*. Translated by Ricard Howard. Hill and Wang, New York.

Barthes, Roland. 1977. *Fragments d'un Discours Amoureux*. Editions du Seuil, Paris.

Barthes, Roland. 1979. *A Lover's Discourse: Fragments*. Translated by Richard Howard Jonathan Cape, London.

Barthes, Roland. 1992. *Incidents*. Translated by Richard Howard. University of California Press, Berkeley.

Billig, Michael.1987. The Art of Witcraft. Ch 5 in *Arguing and Thinking*. Cambridge University Press. Cambridge.

Borges, Jorge Luis. 1970. Pierre Menard, Author of the Quixote. Translated by James E. Irby. From: *Labyrinths*, Penguin, Harmondsworth.

Dervin, Daniel. 1987. Roland Barthes: The Text as Self; The Self as Text. In; *Psychoanalytic Review*. vol. 74, 2, pp. 281-292.

Donnelly, Colleen. 1985. The Non-Homogeneous I: Fragmentation, Desire, and Pleasure in Barthes's A Lover's Discourse. In: *Southern Review*, vol. 21, 2, pp. 169-180.

Gane, Mike. 1980. Borges: Menard: Spinoza. In: Economy and Society, vol. 9, 4. 404-419.

Merquior, José Guilherne. 1985. A Hedonist Apostasy: the Later Barthes. In: *Portuguese Studies*, vol. 1, pp. 182-192.

Mitlitsch, Robert. 1983. Difference: Roland Barthes's *Pleasure of the Text, Text of Pleasure*. In: *Boundary*, 2, vol. 12, pp 101-114.

Contents II

1. *s'abimer*/ to be engulfed. [Kigo: abyss]
2. *affirmation*/ affirmation. [affair]
3. *alteration*/ alteration. [devoted]
4. *angoisse*/ anxiety. [chosen]
5. *casé*/ pigeonholed. [weep]
6. *attente*/ waiting. [dream]
7. *annulation*/ annulment. [excluded]
8. *circonscrire*/ to circumscribe. [rendezvous]
9. *coeur*/ heart [conceal]
10. *comblement*/ fulfilment. [fulfilment]
11. *compassion*/ compassion. [phallos]
12. *comprendre*/ to understand.[make-love]
13. *conduit*/ behaviour. [time]
14. *connivance*/ connivance. [to lead]
15. *contingences*/ contingencies. [carrel]
16. *corps*/ body.[id]
17. *dédicace*/ dedication. [it]
18. *demons*/ demons. [pick]
19. *dépense*/ expenditure.[travel]
20. *déréalité*/ disreality. [jealousy]
21. *écoché*/ flayed. [missing]
22. *écrire*/ to write. [spiral]
23. *étreinte*/ embrace. [off]

24. *exil*/ exile. [thown]
25. *fâcheux*/ irksome. [apology]
26. *inconnaissable*/ unknowable. [the other]
27. *insupportable*/ unbearable. [colloque]
28. *issues*/ outcomes. [sumptuous]
29. *je-t'-aime*/ I-love-you. [syntax]
30. *langueur*/ languor. [menu]
31. *loquela*/ the loquela. [orgy]
32. *mutisme*/ silence [the grain]
33. *nuages*/ clouds. [passionate]
34. [adventure]
35 [pact]
36. [sex]
37. [competition]
38. [legs]
39 [kiss]
40. [voyeur/ voyeuse]
41 [rules]
42. [acosmic]
43. *nuages*/ clouds. [life]
44. *nuit*/ night. [death]
45. *objets*/ objects.[ecstasy]
46. *obscene*/ obscene. [text]
47. *pleurer*/ crying. [duel]
48. *pourquoi*/ why. [abandoned]
49. *regretted*/ regretted. [return]
50. *retentissement*/ reverberation. [memory]
51. *réveil*/ waking. [scatter]
52. *seul*/ alone. [haiku]
53. [You]

The End